Chisholm Trail Showdown

For the young men in the Texas town of Indian Falls, riding the Chisholm Trail as cowboys is a rite of passage which no boy should miss out. 17-year-old Dan Lewis is heartbroken when it looks as though he is to be cheated of his chance to ride the range.

Determinedly, he manages to secure a place on the trail, but Dan is unaware of more sinister powers at play, and his joy quickly fades as he finds himself accused of cattle rustling and nearly lynched as a consequence.

Dan must fight to clear his name, no matter how arduous that might be. He finds himself up against a gang of the most ruthless men in the state, facing a fight more intense than he could have ever imagined.

Can Dan overcome the most important battle of his life?

Chisholm Trail Showdown

Jack Tregarth

A Black Horse Western

ROBERT HALE · LONDON

© Jack Tregarth 2015
First published in Great Britain 2015

ISBN 978-0-7198-1627-7

Robert Hale Limited
Clerkenwell House
Clerkenwell Green
London EC1R 0HT

www.halebooks.com

Typeset by
Derek Doyle & Associates, Shaw Heath
Printed and bound in Great Britain by
CPI Antony Rowe, Chippenham and Eastbourne

CHAPTER 1

It was, thought Dan Lewis, the worst thing ever to befall him in all his seventeen years. Nothing crueller or more unjust was ever likely to happen to him in the future, either. Every spring, most of the young men from in and around the little Texan town of Indian Falls signed up to ride as cowboys; herding cattle north along the Chisholm Trail to the railheads at Abilene, Elsworth and Dodge City. Even if they only went on that arduous journey once, before settling down to work on their fathers' farms or in their stores, it was pretty well accepted that riding as a cowboy was something every red-blooded boy in those parts had to do, if only on a single occasion.

Dan had waited eagerly for the time when he would be old enough to sign up with the big cattle company so that he too could experience the rigours and excitement of life on the trail. Only then could any youngster from thereabouts claim to be a real man. And now, he was to be cheated of this longed-for ambition – the one thing in his whole life that he had most wanted.

The blow had fallen from a blue sky, without any warning at all, when his mother had announced casually over breakfast, 'I reckon you're a-goin' to have to forget about riding the trail this year, Danny boy.'

'What d'you mean, Ma?' he had answered, a sick feeling welling up in the pit of his stomach, like he'd been kicked or punched.

'That hired man of ours was detained last night by Sheriff Rider. Seems as he's wanted for some foolishness, away over in New Mexico. Lord knows what it might be, but I surely can't run this place without either him or you.'

'But, Ma,' said Dan, despite his age, his eyes almost filling with tears, 'I got to go this year. Everybody I know's goin' to be riding out in the next few weeks. I can't be the only one left behind.'

'Well, I can tell you for now,' said his mother firmly, 'there's no question of it and you might as well settle yourself to the fact.'

It has to be said that Mrs Maud Lewis was not a hard-hearted woman, nor was she unaware of the disappointment which her only child was suffering. Still and all, their smallholding wouldn't run itself and the only way that she had managed to keep food on the table since her husband had died seven years earlier was by engaging a series of hired men.

This was expensive, though, and in the last three or four years she had relied increasingly upon her son doing a man's work around the farm. She could just about cope with the place without him, always providing she had somebody to help out every day, but not now the latest fellow had upped and got himself arrested.

Seeing that her son was about to launch into a long and passionate justification, Mrs Lewis decided that the kindest thing would be to let him know right now that there was no chance of his riding off. It wasn't to be thought of, particularly at that time of year, with so much to do in the fields. She said, 'I ain't about to debate further with you, Daniel. I'm tellin' you how it is and that's the way of it. I won't hear another word on the subject.'

'It ain't fair,' cried Dan. 'It just ain't fair!'

'What's fair got to do with the case?' asked his mother.

Before the week was out, Dan Lewis's friends began signing up with the South Texas Livestock Company and leaving town. Danny watched despairingly as the boys he had attended school with went off on their adventures, while he was left to weed fields and tend to the hogs. A phrase that the preacher had used in church the week before struck Dan most powerfully and just about summed up how he felt: 'The iron entered his soul.'

He felt bereft and abandoned, left out of the fun and excitement that most every other fellow of his age for fifty miles was taking part in.

The only other young man of his age in town who had not left within a fortnight was Albert McCormack; a mean and sneaking youth, whose chief claim to fame at the school which he had attended with Dan was his tendency to bear tales to the teacher. Nobody much liked McCormack or wanted to ride alongside him and so he and Danny were pretty much the only young men of sixteen or seventeen to been seen on the streets of Indian Falls that spring.

Now, although the South Texas Livestock Company was the outfit for which most boys in town worked, there was another company, based some twenty miles from Indian Falls. This was generally known for convenience as the Three Cs or the Triple C, on account of its official title being the Carmichael Cattle Company which was obviously something of a mouthful. Two days after the last of his friends had decamped to join the South Texas Livestock Company on their round-up and drive north, two things happened, which together changed the course of Dan Lewis's life forever. The first of these was that a hobo fetched up on the farm, looking for food and shelter, in return for which he was prepared to undertake any work which might be needful about the Lewis small-holding.

'It surely is a pity,' remarked Maud Lewis to her son, 'that this fellow didn't happen by a week or two back.'

'You might say so, Ma!' replied Dan ruefully. At that moment, he caught sight of a rider heading towards them from the little track leading to town. This proved to be the second important circumstance to chance that day, because the rider was none other than Albert McCormack, for whom, like so many others in the district, Dan had little time. He and his mother greeted the boy politely, but without any great cordiality.

'Good morning, Mrs Lewis,' said Albert. 'Hey, Dan.'

'How might we help you, Albert?' asked Dan's mother.

'Well, it ain't so much you helping me,' said the youth. 'I'd say the boot's all on the other foot, so to speak.'

'Oh?' said Mrs Lewis, raising a quizzical eyebrow. 'How's that?'

'I hear the Triple C are plumb desperate to find a couple of likely lads to act as wranglers when they set off tomorrow. My ma wondered if there was any chance of Dan being free now to go on the trail? She don't like the notion o' my ridin' twenty miles over to the Three Cs by myself.'

Dan looked across to his mother, a sudden, wild hope erupting in his heart. Maud Lewis smiled at the eager young man and said slowly, 'Well, seeing as how we have a body now who says he will stay for a month or more and seems a good worker into the bargain, I suppose you might as well go off. It's tolerable clear to me, I'll not be left in peace else.'

Dan rushed up to his mother and enfolded her in a crushing bear-hug. He said, 'Thank you. I'll work twice as hard when I get back.'

'See that you do,' she said gruffly. 'Now get along with you and pack. If you're aiming to get to the Three Cs by nightfall, you'd best move yourself.'

So it came about that on a bright, sunny morning in May 1870, two young men left Indian Falls on their horses heading north towards the headquarters of the Carmichael Cattle Company. They were an ill-matched pair, with neither having much liking or regard for the other and having been thrown together only by chance.

Dan Lewis and Albert McCormack were greeted warmly when they showed up at the Three Cs. It would be stretching the case to claim that the trail boss threw his arms around them and embraced them as he would some long-lost relatives, but there was not the slightest doubt that he was mightily relieved to see two capable-looking youngsters ride in and announce their readiness to start work that very minute if need be. Without a couple of wranglers, it was hard to see how they would have been able to set out with the seven thousand head of cattle that they hoped to despatch to Elsworth.

Texas had, for some years, been heaving to bursting point with steers. They were a positive drug on the market in that state and the price they fetched for their owners was accordingly so low as to make profit margins very tight indeed. All this changed when the railroads began running from Kansas to the East. It then became possible to drive the herds up to railheads in Kansas and transport them by railroad trains to Chicago and other cities. Overnight, the Texas cattle business boomed and this led to the creation of the so-called cow towns of Abilene, Elsworth and Dodge: the ultimate destinations of the steers being driven a thousand miles north from Texas.

Life on the trail was rough and hard. Naturally, the least pleasant tasks ended up being allotted to the youngest and least experienced of the men working the herds. The dirtiest jobs, and the loneliest, were allocated to sixteen- and seventeen-year-olds like Dan Lewis. The post that many of these young men ended up in was that of wrangler.

A lot of nonsense was later written about the strong bond formed between cowboys and their horses. This overlooked the fact that the average cowboy on the trail did not have just one horse which was his own and to which he became attached. It was essential that the horses had adequate periods of rest, even if the riders themselves were sometimes in the saddle for twelve or eighteen hours at a stretch. This apparent paradox was resolved by ensuring that every cowboy had at least three horses during a cattle drive. This in turn meant that there might be as many as a hundred

11

and fifty horses at any one time which were not being ridden. These had to be cared for and looked after carefully, so that there were always fresh mounts ready and waiting for those who needed them. The man in charge of these spare horses was called the wrangler and he was invariably the youngest and greenest man of them all. On a big cattle drive, such as that being undertaken by the Three Cs, more than one wrangler might be needed; which was what had given Dan Lewis his great opportunity that spring.

'You boys best show me your stuff,' said Jethro Carmichael, when they had introduced themselves and stated their purpose in having made their way to his uncle's ranch. 'Nobody'll thank me for sending off a couple o' greenhorns who can't handle theyselves on the trail.'

'What would you have us do, sir?' asked Dan.

'There's a half-dozen lively ponies over in the field yonder. Why don't you and your partner round 'em up and bring 'em into that there corral?'

Surprisingly, Dan found that he and Albert McCormack worked pretty well together as a team. He had never really cared for the fellow, but had to admit that he knew how to handle animals. The horses that Carmichael had told them to fetch into the corral were barely domesticated animals from the Lord knew where. At a guess, Dan thought that they might have been acquired from the Indians. They were as skittish as you liked and not at all used

12

to being chivvied about like this. He hoped devoutly that these critters weren't typical of the horses that he would be expected to tend to for the thousand-mile drive up into Kansas. The six of them were trouble enough in themselves; how he would manage a hundred such animals was something of a mystery to him. This was not going to be the case though, as he later learned. The Triple C bought half-wild creatures like this from time to time and they always got new men to show what they could do with such unpromising material.

After he and Albert had got the ponies penned up in the corral, Jethro Carmichael said, 'Well, you could o' done that a mite quicker, I reckon, but seein' as we're desperate, I suppose you boys will have to do. A dollar a day 'til we reach Elsworth suit you?'

Dan was surprised to hear that they would be receiving the same pay as the other, more experienced men. Thirty dollars a month was the standard rate for cowboys on the trail and he rejoiced to discover that he, too, would be earning this sum. Why, after two months, he would have sixty dollars or thereabouts!

Now that the Three Cs had a full complement of hands, there was no reason to delay the departure any further. It was accordingly agreed that they would set off at dawn the next day. Before he and Albert settled down to sleep in one of the bunkhouses, Dan Lewis took a turn round the ranch. It was, in a way, a solemn kind of moment. He was, as he very well knew, little more than a boy. Once he had ridden a thousand miles in the saddle and helped shift some thousands of longhorns across the country for a couple of months or so, he would return changed; if not yet a man, then certainly nearer to it than was currently the case.

The two boys were woken the next day at dawn by the clanging of a length of rail being beaten vigorously with a metal bar. Dan, Albert and the other ten fellows in the bunkhouse were roused to consciousness by the sharp, metallic clash of iron on iron and the roaring of the foreman, who yelled irritably, 'Come on, you lazy cows' sons, get your asses out o' them bunks. There's work as needs doin'!'

The sun was not yet peeping above the horizon and outside it was chilly and the darkness was inky black. There wasn't much by way of breakfast, other than black coffee which was almost as thick as soup. The two boys soon realized that they would have to figure out for themselves what they were expected to do; all the others were too busy with their own tasks to spend time explaining what was required. Fortunately, it was fairly easy to tell when they got things wrong, because there was yelling and cursing. Somehow, the two of them managed to find the horses and get them ready to move.

There was nothing in the slightest degree romantic about any of the chores being undertaken that first day; it was just damned hard work. By the end of the day, the expedition was under way, though, with better than seven thousand longhorn steers having been rounded up and by and large persuaded to move in the same direction. Dan had always thought of himself as a pretty tough and wiry individual, capable of putting in a good day's work when the need arose. By nightfall, though, he was utterly spent and looking forward to collapsing on the ground, huddling up in his blanket and falling asleep. That was when he learned that he and Albert were in a different category from the other men and would, in a sense, be working through the night as well.

'Here's the way of it, you boys,' explained the trail boss, a man called Geoff Lennox. 'Some of they steers'll be after wandering off in the night. You got the horses secured, I'll allow, but your work ain't ended yet. After you got some vittles in you, you two got to go off different ways and set yourselves down about a mile or more out from here. You can doze all you like, but you keep half an eye open for any cattle which are thinking of taking off in the night. It'll be your job to send 'em back in again.'

And so, while the other forty men were settling down to chat and play cards around the campfires, Dan Lewis rode off alone to set watch over the steers on the edge of the herd. He had no idea how much sleep he was expected to snatch while watching the herd. In the event, Dan found that any sort of

unrest among the steers caused lowing and restless-
ness that was communicated among the herd by
stamping hoofs. Even when he was sound asleep,
the vibrations of this activity roused him.

Sometimes, when the steers were especially rest-
less and nervous, Dan found he could calm those
nearest to him by singing the songs that his mother
had used to soothe him when he was a little child.
Anybody who had happened to be where Dan Lewis
was trying to snatch a few hours' sleep would have
been entertained by the sight and sound of a young
man crooning a series of lullabies to a bunch of
longhorn cattle.

The days and nights wore away in this fashion,
until they had been on the trail for nearly a week;
the herd could not be induced to travel more than
fifteen or twenty miles at most in the course of a day.
And after five days of this back-breaking work,
which left Dan Lewis with more aches than he had
ever had in his life, they was still fewer than a
hundred miles from home.

Now, a natural consequence of the way of life that
Dan and Albert were living on the trail was that they
had little chance to get to know the men with whom
they were working. They caught glimpses of them
during the day, but there was little enough time to
socialize when they were all working. It was in the
evenings that the men chatted together and this was
the part of the day that the boys missed out on. Dan
found this annoying, but he could not in a million

years have guessed that it would put his very life in hazard.

On the sixth night, everything seemed as quiet as could be and Dan was allowing himself to hope that he might be able to hunker down to an uninter- rupted night's sleep. The steers were settled down nicely and so Dan Lewis wrapped himself up in his blanket and lay down on a patch of ground which he had cleared of stones. He was just about to drift off to sleep when he felt the vibration of hoof beats and was jerked back to consciousness.

Once he was sitting up, Dan found that he could hear the hoofs and they didn't sound like the random and irregular pattern of cattle shifting to and fro. It was rather the regular, rhythmic drum- ming of horses' hoofs and unless he was very much mistaken, they were heading his way. He shrugged off the blanket and got to his feet – peering out into the darkness to see who was coming. It seemed to him that there were at least two horses coming towards him and he wondered who could be looking for him at that time of night.

CHAPTER 2

It was a moonless night and Dan Lewis could barely make out the silhouettes of the two horsemen who were coming along in his direction, but when he judged that they were within hailing distance, he cupped his hands to his mouth and cried, 'Hey there, what's to do?'

The riders whirled round and cantered up to him. One of the men said, 'You the wrangler setting a watch on these critters?'

'That I am.'

'We gotta peel off a hundred and move 'em aways down the valley there. Boss said as you'd help us.'

'How's that? Why'd you be wanting to take a hundred from here and move them over there? It don't make sense!'

'Hell, I'm just doin' as I been bid. You going to help or hinder?'

'Wait 'til I got my boots on and my horse tacked up.'

Because he hadn't really had any opportunity to get to know by sight any of the men riding with the herd, Dan simply took it for granted that these two men must be cowboys sent by Lennox to undertake some job or other. He pulled on his boots and then readied his pony for work. It was, he thought, a bit thick to disturb his rest in this way and think that he would simply jump into the saddle and get working in the middle of the night. Still and all, they were paying him a dollar a day and feeding him into the bargain, so he figured that he ought to do as he had been instructed.

'You want any particular steers?' asked Dan helpfully. 'Or just the first hundred we come across?'

'Shit,' said one of the men with a laugh. 'You think I'm a-goin' to get down and examine the beasts? Let's us just get us a hundred of these bastards and be done with it.'

Together, the three of them managed to round up a hundred head of cattle without spooking the rest of the herd unduly; no mean feat in the dark. It struck Dan that these men really knew their stuff. They were able to soothe the longhorns, not by singing lullabies to them or any of that foolishness, but rather by making reassuring noises in their throats. It was wonderful to behold, the way that these fellows were able to control the steers and stop the movements of a few turning into a general stampede or something of that nature.

The three of them were doing famously and had

19

separated out the hundred that they wanted and were herding them off, away from the others, when a dozen men on horseback rode down on them and ordered them all to throw down their guns. Some of the riders were carrying blazing pine brands and the flickering light lent them an eldritch aspect, the lengthy shadows making them look like hobgoblins or ghosts. At first, Dan thought that these new men might be outlaws or rustlers. He couldn't for the life of him work out why they would otherwise be troubling three men peacefully engaged in herding cattle. Then, to his consternation, he saw that the party of men was led by Geoff Lennox, the trail boss. Dan himself didn't have a gun, but the two men he had been helping did and they threw down the pistols that they were carrying. 'Now you all get down from your horses,' ordered Lennox, 'and don't any of you make any sudden moves.'

As though in a dream, Dan dismounted, quite unable to work out the play. Then Geoff Lennox spoke again. He said, 'You men know what you done and you know what's comin' to you.' He looked hard at Dan and said, 'And you, boy, you took up with us, ate our food and all just to start rustlin' our cattle soon as you could. I don't know as that's not worst of all, worse than these men.'

'Rustlin'?' exclaimed Dan in astonishment. 'Who's been rustlin'? I was given word as you wanted me to help these fellows fetch a hundred head out the herd.'

Lennox smiled grimly, saying, 'That's a good story. You save your breath, boy, you're likely to need it directly.'

The significance of this observation quite escaped Dan Lewis and he thought he'd wait until they were back at the main camp before he explained the ins and outs of the matter. Nobody at present seemed inclined to listen to what he had to say.

It was not apparently Lennox's intention to head back to camp. The dismounted men were shep-herded instead towards a small wood which spread out on one side of the track leading to the valley. Dan still didn't understand what was going on and it wasn't until they halted by a tall oak and one of the riders sent a coil of rope snaking over a low branch that the peril he was in suddenly grasped Dan Lewis's heart in an icy grip. They were going to lynch him!

'Hey, you can't do this!' shouted Dan, his voice quavering in terror. 'I ain't done nothing.'

'You call signing up for a drive and then throwing in with rustlers as nothing?' asked Lennox. 'You and me got different views on that subject. Tie their hands.'

Dan and the other two men struggled, but to no avail; in two minutes, all three of them had their hands firmly bound behind their backs with rawhide thongs. In the meantime, two more ropes had been thrown over the branches of the oak tree

21

and nooses fashioned at their ends. 'Get them on their horses!' commanded the trail boss. Dan Lewis dug his feet into the ground like a mule, but found himself being inexorably pushed and pulled towards the waiting ropes. He saw that he was being dragged past old Jack Trotter, the man in charge of the chuck wagon. He appealed to him.

'Mr Trotter, I ain't done aught I shouldn't've! I was sitting up there, minding my own affairs when those two men rode up. I swear I thought they was working for this outfit.'

'Get them up on their horses,' repeated Lennox. Dan saw that their horses had been brought along and positioned under the three nooses which now dangled from the tree. He felt almost sick with fear and was on the point of weeping, when Jack Trotter interrupted the proceedings. He came over to Dan and said:

'How old are you, son?'

'I was seventeen this March gone.'

Now although Geoff Lennox was the trail boss and nominally in charge of the whole enterprise, old Jack Trotter's word counted for a good deal. He might be the cook now, but he was also a dab-hand at medical matters and had been working for the Triple C longer than most any of the other men. He turned to Lennox and said, 'He's no more than a boy. No matter what he's done, we can't hang a body of that age.'

At first, Lennox looked to Dan as though he was

inclined to argue the point, but then he said, 'Ah, let the little bastard alone, then. But mind you make him watch what happens.'

Two of the cowboys gripped Dan's shoulders and made sure that he couldn't turn away. The two men who had got him mixed up in all this were hoisted and manhandled on to their horses. The ropes were adjusted round their necks and then everybody stepped aside from them. In the light of the pine torches, it appeared to Dan that they were defiant and not in the least afraid.

'You men knew what to expect if'n you was caught at this game,' said Lennox. 'Rustlin'll get you hanged most anywhere. Either of you got anything to say for yourselves?'

Dan wondered if they would take this opportunity to admit that he himself had been innocent of any involvement in what they had been up to; but they neither of them spoke. Then Lennox nodded to the others and two men stepped forward and gave the horses sharp slaps across the rump. They jerked forward, leaving their riders suspended in mid-air. Both of the men kicked and danced for a spell on the end of their ropes. They died hard.

After it was all over and the men were dead, Lennox came over to where Dan stood and said, 'You was damned lucky that Jack here spoke out for you. I would o' just hanged you, had it been left to me. You took our food and then betrayed us.'

Jack Trotter said, 'I'm right disappointed in you,

son. I took you to be a straight one and I own now as I was wrong about it. You go off now and thank your stars as you're still alive.' He turned away before Dan had a chance to say anything.

Nobody wanted to hear anything that Dan had to say. When he began speaking, they just turned and walked off in disgust. It was obvious that every man present thought that he had signed up with their outfit as a pretext for being involved in the theft of cattle. None of these men knew him; it wasn't like it would have been had he been riding with the South Texas Livestock Company. Had that been the case, then he would have had any number of men who had known him for years who would have been ready to speak up for him. Here, he was a stranger. Sadly, although conscious that he had narrowly escaped with his life, Dan Lewis mounted his pony and rode off into the night.

It was impossible to say what time it was. Dan thought that it was after midnight, although he couldn't be sure about it. The question was: what was he to do now? There were, it seemed to the young man, only two possibilities. The first was that he turned his horse south and made his way straight back to Indian Falls. This was not an appetizing prospect. He would be called upon to explain himself and tell folks why he was back so soon. Now, although most people in town would take his part and readily believe that he had been misjudged, Dan knew also that there would be others who would be eager to believe the worst about him. He had in the past seen what happened to men who had been under suspicion for acts of dishonesty. Even when everybody assured them to their faces that they didn't believe a word of the accusations made against them, there would always be whispers circulating to the effect that there was no smoke without fire.

Then again, he thought, there was little point in returning to his home town and dreaming up some tall tale to account for his coming home after little more than a week. Trying to conceal the truth would only make things worse in the end. Albert McCormack would be certain-sure to spread the truth about his ignominious departure from the trail, far and wide as soon as he came back to Indian Falls himself. Such a course of evasion would only serve to make things look all the blacker for Dan in the long run.

It was at this point that Dan Lewis reined in his horse and realized what he had been doing. He'd been trying to work out a way of wriggling out of this trouble and making sure that folks didn't think too badly of him. But that was all just plumb crazy; he hadn't done anything he need feel ashamed of and so why the devil should he be worrying about looking bad? Away over in the distance, he could hear the soft lowing of the cattle. He needed to put a bit more space between him and that herd yet. It wouldn't do, come sun-up, to still be in that area.

The sheer injustice of the thing rankled in the young man's breast. He had always been as straight as a die and now this! Well, he would have to use his brains if he intended to clear his name. Dan dismounted and paced up and down, reasoning the matter out in his mind. Clearly, those two fellows he had seen hanged had been aiming to take a hundred head of cattle away somewhere. Surely though, they wouldn't have been able to keep those steers with them for long – not just the two of them. There must be others in this racket. And a hundred wasn't all that many. Most of the drives north were of three thousand or more longhorns. Compared to that, a hundred was nothing at all. Whatever was going on, this evening's actions could only be a small part of it.

I guess, thought Dan Lewis to himself, that the best bet is for me to follow along after the Triple C and find out what's what. It'll be a dangerous game, because when all's said and done, I only narrowly escaped being hanged less than an hour since. Still and all, I can't think of a better scheme right now. Maybe something will come to my mind during the night. Scripture says that, 'morning brings counsel', which is just another way of saying that things often look better after a night's sleep. When he woke the next day, Dan Lewis found that he was quite fixed in his purpose, which was to follow the cattle drive at a discreet distance and see what would chance. It wasn't a brilliant plan, but it was, it seemed to the

26

boy, better than nothing.

Sometimes, real life can be stranger than fiction and the next day proved the truth of this adage. Dan made sure that he kept a good four, maybe five, miles back from the drive. There was no danger of losing track of the herds entirely: the clouds of dust they raised made it possible to track their progress at a good deal further than just four miles.

Now, there are a number of men on a cattle drive who ride point, rounding up stray steers and setting a watch for any stragglers. These men still keep as close to the herds as is practical, though. As he rode along that morning, Dan Lewis became aware that there were other riders taking an interest in the Three Cs' progress. He spotted two such men and gained the distinct impression that, like him, they were anxious not to be seen. At first, he thought that they might just be riding point, but he soon saw that they were keeping too far from the herd to be accomplishing any such purpose.

After observing them narrowly over the course of several hours, Dan became convinced that these two other riders were not just random travellers who happened to be following the same route north. They were, like him, following the herd for some reason. Confirmation of his suspicions came a little after noon, when he caught a flash of light from one of the riders ahead of him. He saw the sunlight winking back and forth. Dan had no doubt that this man was communicating with his partner by means of a piece of mirror: flashing signals by reflecting the sunlight across the valley. The only question now was what these fellows were up to.

Young Dan was not a cunning sort of youth – quite the opposite. Even so, he could see that this was not an occasion where being open and honest would be the best plan. It wasn't plain to him whether or not the men following the Triple C would have spotted him. If he'd seen them, then he supposed that like as not, they would have seen him. Were they as curious about him as he was about them? While he wrestled with this conundrum, Dan had a wholly unlooked-for stroke of good fortune.

The land was gently undulating, although there was high ground to either side of the path that the cattle drive was taking. The two mysterious riders were keeping up on the sides of the wide, shallow valley, while Dan was pretty much dogging the heels of the cattle; following almost in their very hoof prints. Now, one of the regular hazards of riding the trail was being caught up in a stampede. This could be very dangerous and it was by no means unknown for men to lose their lives in the process. Usually, great efforts were made to retrieve the bodies of those who suffered this death and to give them Christian burials. Every so often, though, it chanced that a man met his death under the hoofs of several thousand longhorns and the fact was not marked by his fellows; in effect, he simply vanished.

Since men abandoned their posts from time to time for various reasons, a man suddenly and without warning disappearing from sight was not at all unknown.

It was the glint of metal in the bright, morning sun which first caught Dan's attention. He stopped to see what might be lying there in the poached-up and brick-hard mud. Whatever it was was buried in the ground and must have been there for some good long time as this object was embedded in caked earth. Like as not, it had been there for at least a few weeks, since last it was rainy and wet around here.

Although he was in a hurry and keen to find out about the two riders, Dan dismounted and began to investigate. He reached down and prodded the earth. To his immense horror and disgust, a clod of dried soil fell away to reveal a man's half-decayed face. He recoiled in shock, before recollecting that he was no longer some little child who was scared of the bogeyman, but rather a grown person, riding the range alone.

The shiny metal that had first caught his eye turned out to be a pistol and to Dan's amazement, it appeared to be in good working order. It was a Navy Colt and from all that he was able to collect, it was fully loaded. Most of it had been covered by dried mud, but once he had prised it loose and shaken the dirt from it, there seemed to be nothing wrong with the weapon. Leastways, the cylinder spun smoothly and the hammer cocked without any difficulty. It was a miracle that all those steers had trampled over the ground here without doing the pistol a mischief.

The body of the pistol's owner was almost entirely buried and looked to have been squashed almost flat. How this gun had survived was a mystery, the answer to which he would probably never know. There were even caps over the nipples of the cylinder and he could see balls as well – each neatly secured in one of the five chambers. Would it fire? Well, that would remain to be seen. The way things were panning out, Dan had an idea that it would not be too long until he found out the answer to that question.

The boy felt a twinge of bad conscience at looting a dead body in this way. However, he soon recollected himself and realized that a dead man had no use for firearms and that if he left the gun there, then it would surely be picked up by the next traveller to pass this way. 'Sides which, he had great need for that pistol. As a compromise, Dan recited a prayer over the man's remains and wished him into heaven and not the other place.

After tucking the pistol in his belt, Dan thought to himself that there was little point in fooling around any further. He had no food, only a dollar fifty in cash and no other plan beyond following the Triple C herd until something turned up. Well, maybe it was time to make things happen. He mounted and then spurred on his horse, heading up towards the higher ground, where one of the riders he had seen earlier was to be found.

It took fifteen minutes to catch up with the rider and when the man became aware that Dan was bearing down on him, he reined in and turned to face the youngster. Dan saw that he was carrying not one but two pistols, in low-slung black holsters. When Dan was almost upon him, the fellow said in a friendly enough way, 'Whoa now, that's about close enough, boy. What are you about?'

'I been thrown out of yon company and I'm lookin' for work.'

The man, who was so dark-skinned as to cause Dan to wonder if he was perhaps Mexican, said, 'This is strange listening. Why should you think as I might give you a job?'

'Well, I'm thinking you might be vexed with those whores' sons for doing harm to your friends.'

Dan very seldom used strong language and wondered for a second if he was overdoing his tough act. Apparently not, because the man started in surprise and said, 'Who are these friends of mine?'

'The ones who tried to make off with a hundred steers yester eve,' said Dan confidently. 'You say you're nothing' to do with the case?'

'What harm's befallen them?'

'They was hanged last night.'

'The hell they were! Who did that?'

Dan had worked out the story as he rode up and,

31

although he was not a practised or adept liar, he had an instinctive feel for weaving together just enough truth with his tale to invite belief. He was quite sure now that the man he was talking to was an associate of the men he had seen killed yesterday. This in turn meant that he might be able to use this fellow to lead him to those who had been responsible for nearly getting him hanged along with the two rustlers. He said, 'Here's the way of it. I been caught sleeping on watch a couple of times and the trail boss said as if it happened one more time, then he'd hoof me out and I wouldn't get paid. Well, sure enough, last night he come upon me, sound asleep. He was in such a temper that I feared for my safety. He says, "You bastard cowson, you. Just get yourself out of here." Just then, his men came up and they'd caught two men stealin' stock. He caused 'em to be strung up and then he threw me out the place and well, here I am.'

'You sure they dead?'

'Sure I'm sure. I see 'em hang, like I done told you.'

'That's the hell of a thing. They was good friends to me.'

'Well, I'm looking for work. You reckon as you could use me?'

The other man stared at Dan, eyeing him up and down, thoughtfully. At length, he said, 'It may be so.'

CHAPTER 3

Dave Carson had been running a herd of longhorns since he was a young man in the early forties; at about the same time that others, like Ezra Carmichael, were also grubbing a living out of raising cattle purely for the consumption of those living in Texas. It had been a struggle in those days to make a decent living out of that kind of farming and so Carson had let that side of his business fall off and had concentrated on growing crops instead. That too had failed, the barren soil of southern Texas not being suited to the growing of wheat and barley. By the time that Dan Carson had realized his mistake, the cattle market had picked up and he had been left behind by those who had stuck at it and helped set up the trails to Kansas taking advantage of the new railroads.

In short, by making a miscalculation in his younger days, Dave Carson had missed out on the chance to become a cattle baron, one of those who became rich through supplying the eastern states with prime quality meat for the workers in the rapidly growing cities. Each year, the smaller men like Carson found themselves getting squeezed just a little more by the big operations such as the Carmichael Cattle Company and the South Texas Livestock Company.

As the years passed, all this rankled with Carson and he began to persuade himself that he had, in some obscure way, been cheated. As his own fortunes waned and those of men like Carmichael waxed ever stronger, Dave Carson's mind turned to thoughts of revenge. Why should those men have all the luck and all the riches associated with the livestock business, while he contented himself with the crumbs from their tables?

The War Between the States was a turning point, because of course the southern army was desperate for meat to feed its men on. The Three Cs and the South Texas Livestock Company won contracts to supply the army, while Carson was ignored and saw his own herds slaughtered and sold at a pittance for the local market. By the end of the war in 1865, his ranch was like a ghost town. It was then, at the lowest point of his fortunes, that Dave Carson had hit upon the scheme which would both revive his own prosperity and provide him with a convenient way of revenging himself upon those who he blamed for his poverty.

When you are driving between three and ten

thousand head of cattle for a thousand miles, it stands to reason that you are going to lose some of them on the way. They will fall sick, tumble into rivers and drown, crush each other to death, wander off, topple over cliffs or fall victim to a hundred and one other vagaries of chance. You can't count every one of those steers every day on the trail and often it was only when they were being loaded on to the trucks at the railhead in Elsworth that it would be possible to work out just how many had been lost en route from Texas. No matter how much care was taken during the cattle drive, regard-less of how many men were engaged in watching for stragglers there would always be a few hundred fewer steers at the railhead than there were when the journey began back in Texas. Much the same applied to the situation in winter, when the herds were just grazing out on the range. There were always losses between the fall and the springtime. It was this which had given Carson the germ of an idea, five years before Dan Lewis set out on the trail from Indian Falls.

He had begun in a small way in the spring of 1866, by hiring a half-dozen former soldiers who were down on their luck and would do more or less anything for a good meal and a place to stay. In the first instance, Carson had got these fellows to bring him as many mavericks as they could lay hands on before the spring round-up. By tradition, mavericks, which is to say unbranded calves, belonged to nobody and were there for the taking of whoever first chanced upon them. That spring, the men working for Carson managed to bring him nearly two hundred calves which had not yet been branded and so claimed by the owners of their sires. This was when Dan Carson showed that he had a real and hitherto unsuspected flair for crime.

The Three Cs brand was just that: three Cs in row, one after the other. Thinking ahead, to the time that he might want more than a few mavericks and stragglers, Carson officially registered his own brand: the Barred Os. This consisted of three Os, with a long line passing straight through the middle of them all. There was nothing out of the ordinary about this. As the years passed, most of the brands using simple combinations of letters had already been registered and so letters and symbols struck through with a line or bar were becoming increasingly common.

After the Barred Os was registered to him, Dan Carson had sent out two of his boys to bring in one of Carmichael's branded steers. He had carefully measured the Triple C brand and then set a fellow in his forge to tailor a branding iron to precisely those dimensions. The result had exceeded his wildest hopes. When the Barred O brand was applied over the existing mark, it obliterated the three Cs and replaced them with his own three Os with the bar through them. It was absolutely impossible to detect the least hint of a previous brand.

Ezra Carmichael's steer now bore Carson's own brand and he defied anybody in the world to prove that this was not his own property.

Of course, it would not be prudent to prey solely upon the Triple Cs' stock. The brand of the South Texas Livestock Company was just ST. Carson had another brand registered in his own name, which was a figure eight followed by a square with a vertical line running down the middle and dividing it into oblongs. This too could be overlaid on the ST brand, replacing it and making it all but impossible to tell that there had previously been a mark there at all.

Over the course of four years, Carson had built up what was, in effect, a rustling operation on an industrial scale. He stole steers from both the main cattle companies in that part of Texas and simply converted them into his own stock. He was careful not to appear to be doing too well financially, but by the spring of 1870, his was the third largest cattle company in the southern half of the state, after the Three Cs and the South Texas Livestock Company.

The problem is of course that when you are getting something for nothing in this way and simply taking other folks' property willy-nilly as the mood strikes you, you are apt to get a little greedy and careless after a time. This is what had happened in the spring of 1870 and the two men who had been caught and hanged by the trail boss of the Triple C had actually already made one raid on that particular cattle drive, only two nights after they had left the ranch. Carson paid them handsome bonuses for every steer successfully abstracted from his competitors and then the two men had been summarily executed.

Dan Lewis, of course, knew nothing of all this. His only interest in the business was that he had come damned close to losing his own life the previous night and was now regarded as a rustler himself. His sole aim now was to clear his name and show that he was not the sort of sneaking wretch who would sign up with an outfit and then betray them for money.

Once the man to whom Dan was talking felt sure that the other two men that he had evidently been working with were definitely dead, he said nothing more, but took from his saddle-bag a piece of silvered glass which looked to have a small peep-hole scraped in the backing. This he raised to his eye and peered out across the valley with it. Seeing Dan's interest, he told him, 'It's the latest thing in communicating in the field. The British call it a heliograph. I can use it to send messages to my partner, over on the hill yonder.'

'What're you telling him?' asked Dan.

'To come right here so as we can work out what's best to do. You better not be lying about our friends, boy, I'll tell you that for nothing.'

'I ain't lying,' said Dan indignantly. He was struck by a thought. 'Say, if you like, I can lead you back there and show you where they're hanging from a tree still.'

The man pulled a face, like he'd bitten into something sour. 'No,' he said, 'I reckon I'll pass on that. I'll take what you say as a true bill. Lord, I don't want to see any hanged man.'

'You the superstitious kind?' asked Dan with interest.

The suggestion appeared to irk the fellow, for he said irritably, 'It ain't a matter of being superstitious. All of us who live so can end up in that way if we don't take care. I just don't like to be reminded of it overmuch.'

'It's nothing to me,' said Dan, indifferently.

When the man's partner arrived, he listened to what Dan had to say and then swore like a mule skinner. Dan thought that he had heard some cussing and bad language in his time; but this fellow beat all that he had ever encountered before. He swore for several minutes without stopping. When finally he ran out of steam, the other man said, 'Well, then, what's to do?'

'What's to do? Why, we cut for home, of course. It'd be madness to try anything more as things stand now.'

'What of the boy here?'

'He can ride along of us, if he cares to. I dare say as we can find a use for a likely fellow like that, 'specially since he's been riding with Carmichael's outfit.'

So it was that Dan Lewis found himself falling in with a set of the most dangerous and determined rustlers to be found anywhere in Texas at that time.

Careful as Dave Carson had been not to draw undue attention to his newly found success in the cattle business, word had inevitably got around that the man most had written off as a no-count dirt farmer was now flourishing. Carson's spread was tucked out of the way and he did not encourage casual visitors. Even so, there was some suspicion about the means by which he had recovered from almost-ruin and was now being talked of as a big player in the field of livestock. There was a stock growers' association in Texas, to which everybody of consequence in the business of cattle farming belonged. Everybody, that is, except Dave Carson. A month or two earlier, there had been a meeting of this organization, at which it had been agreed that a sum would be set aside to engage the Pinkerton agency to send an investigator down to look into what might be going on at the Carson ranch.

'What age do you have, boy?' asked the first of the men he had picked up with that day. They were riding at an undemanding trot, away from the Three Cs cattle drive and heading, as far as Dan could gauge, south-east.

'I'm seventeen, sir, just gone.'

'Never mind with the "sir", you can call me Lance. This your first ride out like this?'

'Yes. Yes it is.'

40

'I tell you now, you fall asleep on the job with us and it'll be a sight worse than just curse words you'll earn. You like as not figured the play by now. You seem a smart lad. What do you think we're about?'

Dan shrugged with a nonchalance he was far from feeling within. 'Rustling, I guess.'

'You know it's a hanging matter?'

'Everybody knows that. 'Sides which, if I hadn't o' known it before, I would o' done after seeing those friends of yours hanged last night.'

There was silence for a space, as the two other men mulled over the idea of two of their companions being lynched in that way. Then the second of the men, who had introduced himself as 'Fats', said, 'So you know why it's life and death when we're out on the scout. You fall asleep when you're on the lookout for us and it could mean the death of us. We all of us hold the lives of our friends in our hands when we're working. You do well to recollect that.'

All this was alarming enough to the boy, who began to wonder if he hadn't taken a wrong turn by throwing his lot in with such men. Then he thought about the prospect of returning to Indian Falls so soon after leaving and the questions that such a course of action would invite. No, he thought to himself, I better stick at this for the time being. If I can find out a little more about these characters, then it will go some little way towards proving I wasn't guilty myself of rustling.

It looked as though they wouldn't reach their destination that day and Dan was feeling almost faint with hunger – not having eaten since the night before. He didn't like to broach the subject of food, though, lest he appear to be a weakling. As it was, there was no need to do so, because a few hours before twilight, they arrived at a little blind canyon where five other men were waiting for them. When they saw that there were no cattle being driven, there were shouts of irritation and dismay. They all of them pretty much depended on the extra money that was paid for successful raids on the cattle drives.

The man who called himself Fats explained what had happened and thoughts of money were soon overshadowed by the spectre of death. All these men knew the risks that they ran and the prospect of being hanged out of hand was a very real one to them all.

One of the men who had been lying low in the canyon said to Dan, 'How'd they die? Was they brave about it?'

'I never saw anybody seem less troubled at the idea o' being hanged,' replied Dan, truthfully enough. 'They didn't say a word, nor plead for their lives nor anything at all. Just got on with it and accepted it like they might anything else. They were game ones, all right.'

'Ah, I wouldn't've thought anything less of 'em. Pete Barker was born game and so was Jed,' said another man. 'I'd o' guessed that's how they'd die.'

As much as the seven men present seemed to have a deal of respect for the two who had died, their eulogies didn't last long and they soon fell to discussing the more practical matter of how they might best acquire cattle from another source. To Dan's relief, eating was the main concern, though, at that moment and a fire was kindled, so that coffee might be brewed up and some meat broiled. Nobody showed any particular interest in Dan and he formed the impression that stray men were often being picked up by this crew.

After they had eaten, those who had pipes lit them and there was a feeling of relaxation. They might have been disappointed to find that there were no steers to take back to the Carson spread tomorrow, but these were not men who tended to dwell unduly upon past misfortune. They were far more concerned about the present and, seeing that their bellies were now full and there was no short-age of tobacco, they were pretty well content to let the morrow take care of itself.

Next day, all but two of the men set out for Carson's ranch, which seemingly lay a half-day's ride away. Nobody took the least notice of Dan Lewis for which he was profoundly grateful. It gave him the opportunity to ravel threads of his own and dream up a suitable story for when they arrived at their des-tination.

The six of them reached Dave Carson's place at

about four that afternoon. Not one of them saw the man lying on his belly up in the hills surrounding the Carson spread. He surveyed the area constantly with a pair of military field glasses, sweeping them back and forth, looking for the Lord knew what.

Abraham Goldman of the Pinkerton agency was not a happy man. He was essentially a city dweller. Set him down in the meanest Chicago street and you could be sure that if there was any species of villainy about, Goldman would be the one to sniff it out and expose it. The open range was something else again, though, and as he lay there, scanning the buildings and fields of Dave Carson's ranch, Goldman wondered what on earth he was supposed to be looking for. It was easy enough to spot a crooked faro table or some bent operation; knowing the signs that would distinguish a dishonest cattle dealer from one who was a straight dealer, though, was something else again. As the riders passed below him, Goldman marked that some were men he had seen before, but that the party also included a young man he didn't know.

'We'll take you to see Mr Carson,' said the man whom Dan had first met. 'He'll say if you can work here or not.'

'What's he like?' asked Dan curiously.

'You've no need to be afeared of him, if that's what you're askin'. He's a decent man.'

This struck Dan Lewis as an odd way of describing a man who was in charge of a large rustling operation, but he said nothing. In truth, he was thinking only of how swiftly he might be able to gather enough information about these rascals and then inform on them to the nearest sheriff's office. So far, he had only heard a lot of gossip. He'd a notion that if the law got involved, then they would want hard evidence before they would take action.

Carson liked the look of the young fellow that Fats and his friend had picked up on their travels. He said, 'So you're wanting to team up with us, is that the way of it?'

'If you'll have me, I would.'

'Tell me about yourself, son.'

Dan was able to tell almost the entire truth in answer to this enquiry. He just added a few fanciful touches about being indolent, representing that as the cause of his being thrown out of the drive. When he'd finished spinning his tale, Dave Carson said nothing for a minute or so and then asked what scruples the youth had, if any, about undertaking work which was illegal. 'Got nothing at all in that way,' replied Dan. 'I'll do whatever's needful, you don't have to worry about that.'

'You'll stick at nothing, hey?' said Carson. He slapped the young man on the back and said, 'With an outlook of that sort, I have no doubt that we'll get along famously, my boy. You cut along now to one of the bunkhouses and see where's there room for you.'

To his surprise, Dan found that he was all over

sweat, after his brief interview with the boss of the Barred Os. True, the man had been affability itself when talking to him, but when all was said and done, he and all the others there were engaged in an enterprise which could land them all within the shadow of the rope. How much Dan Lewis's life might be worth if once it was discovered that he was there as a spy and an informer, he really wouldn't have cared to guess.

The men in the bunkhouse where Dan fetched up were a motley bunch. Almost all of them were former soldiers who had, without exception, fought for the Confederacy. None of them were from Texas originally; they had drifted south in hope of escaping the horrors of the Reconstruction. These were men who had been cheated by those they trusted and then treated badly by the set of new masters who popped up after the war. There was a grim camaraderie among them, in which Dan felt unable to share.

Nobody appeared to mind if he just loafed around for the time being; there had been no suggestion that he had been assigned any kind of work yet and so Dan, feeling a little excluded from the group in his bunkhouse, decided to go for a stroll outside.

The Carson spread was an extensive one, covering many hundreds of acres. It might be an idea, thought Dan, to familiarize himself with the layout of the place. He didn't expect to uncover any solid clues about wrongdoing straight away, but it would do no harm at all to know how the place was laid out. He wandered aimlessly over to the forge, noting the branding irons stacked against the wall. There was nobody around, so he entered the smithy and picked up one of the irons and hefted it in his hand. The end was formed of three neat Os and a long line, which ran through them. Dan picked up another branding iron and examined it with interest. This one was of a different design: a figure of eight, next to a square divided in half.

A hand fell on Dan's shoulder and he whirled round to find that the man he knew as Fats was eyeing him with disfavour.

CHAPTER 4

'What in the hell are you doin', poking round here?' said Fats. 'You spyin' on us, maybe?'

The words sent a chill through Dan Lewis's heart and he hoped that he was not about to go red, as he often did when detected in some misdemeanour. 'Spy, yourself!' he said angrily. 'What d'you mean by creepin' up behind a fellow in that wise?'

To Dan's surprise, Fats burst out laughing. 'You got some sand, boy!' he said. 'I didn't mean to accuse you of nothin'. Just wondered what you were up to.'

'Never really had any dealings with branding or aught of that kind,' said Dan. 'I was just thinkin' of how it might be for the steer, was all.'

'They don't feel nothing,' Fats assured him. 'They skin is right tough and thick. The heat only touches the surface. It ain't like it would be if you or me was touched with a red-hot iron. Come along of me and I'll show you how it's done.'

There was something about Fats that Dan found alarming, although he could not for the life of him have said why. On the face of it, the man was friendly enough, but Dan felt in his company that same visceral unease which some experience in the presence of snakes. The man just gave him the creeps.

Fats led Dan to a field which contained ten or twelve unbranded calves. They were frisky little things; weaned, but still full of a babyish love of play. When they saw the two men approaching, three of the calves came gambolling over to greet them. Fats reached over the rail and scratched one of the cute little things behind the ears.

'You know 'bout mavericks?'

'What, you mean those little ones as are found roaming free without marks?' asked Dan. 'Sure, I know it's by way of being a case of finders keepers, as you might say.'

'Well, then, these here are mavericks as me and the boys have found. We've yet to mark 'em, so happen you can lend a hand. We'll do it now.'

'Surely.'

'Listen up, why don't you scoot back to the forge and fetch me a sack o' charcoal. Bring one o' them irons as well: the Barred Os.'

It didn't take long between the two of them to kindle a fire by the side of the field containing the calves. There were plenty of sticks and pieces of dried cow dung around to start off the charcoal.

Once that was going well, Fats placed the iron in the heart of the fire and directed Dan to bring over a calf. Although the little creature reached only a little higher than Dan's waist, it was surprisingly strong and evinced a marked reluctance to come near the fire. It took all Dan's strength to drag the frightened animal to the fire and then wrestle it to the ground. Fats snorted derisively as he saw the delicate way that Dan handled the calves. 'Jeez, man,' he shouted. 'You'll have to work faster than that. What's wrong, you afraid of those beasts?'

'I ain't afraid o' them,' replied Dan indignantly, 'I just don't want to hurt 'em.'

'Hurt 'em? Why, there're a-goin' to be ate in a year or two. Stop being so dainty about it. Listen, you take the branding iron and I'll show you how to bring 'em in.'

Even when he was rounding up the hogs on his own farm, Dan didn't like to see them scared or to be too rough with them. Fats showed no such consideration for the calves, dragging them over to where Dan stood waiting at the fire with many kicks, blows and curses. By the time he knocked them to the ground, the poor things were terrified out of their wits, their eyes staring and their breath coming in short, painful gasps. 'There now,' said Fats. 'You just gotta let 'em know who's boss.'

While he was trying to summon up the courage to place the hot iron against the calf's skin, Dan thought that he caught a glint of light up in the hills which overlooked the fields. It put him in mind of the winking flash which had alerted him to the presence of the men from the Carson ranch, the day before. But when he looked closely to see what had caused the light, he could see nothing. 'What the hell are you gaping at?' enquired Fats sharply. 'Christ, even when I do all the hard work and bring the animals to you, you're still dreaming and gazing off at the Lord knows where. I tell you straight, you stay here and you're goin' to have to liven your ideas up!'

Abe Goldman reached his hand round quickly and covered the lenses of the powerful Zeiss binoculars. The youth had stared straight up at him and Goldman felt sure he'd been spotted. To his relief, the two men he had been observing just carried on with their branding. Had they been suspicious, he guessed that they would have mounted up and ridden into the hills to investigate.

The sight of a dozen or so calves in a corral was enough to arouse the liveliest apprehensions in the mind of the Pinkerton's agent that he had come upon a large-scale rustling operation. That the two men below were in the process of marking those same calves suggested that they were mavericks, which had probably been collected wholesale from the surrounding countryside.

The unwritten rule about mavericks being free for all comers to take and claim for their own was an ancient tradition but one which had now reached the end of its useful life. It was one thing when it might involve the odd stray calf here and there, quite another when gangs of men were combing the land systematically in search of calves, as these fellows evidently had been.

Goldman was an old-fashioned kind of fellow, with a great respect for the customs which had arisen over the frontier years, but he could see that this old tradition was being sorely abused by men such as the owner of the Barred Os. Well, Mr Dave Carson's days at this racket were surely numbered now. As far as Abraham Goldman was concerned, he had enough evidence to make his report. It would then be up to others what to make of it all. At a guess, some of the big ranchers would put together a body of men and ride up here to settle the matter for their own selves. Goldman couldn't see anybody taking the trouble to involve the regular law in something of this sort.

When they had finally got all the calves branded, Fats took Dan over to have coffee with some of the other men whom he had not yet met; they were a rough-looking bunch and no mistake. Indian Falls, like most towns, had one or two inhabitants who were generally known to be shiftless, idle and vicious. One could often recognize these types, by the way that decent and respectable folk tended to give them a wide berth when walking along Main Street. Some such were charity cases, whose neighbours made sure that their families did not suffer too badly as a consequence of the breadwinner's incorrigible disposition. Then again, others were lone wolves: men who lived alone and preyed on whoever they could find. These were men who would steal chickens from the nearest farm or even rustle horses and cattle if the opportunity presented itself.

Hitherto, Dan Lewis had only ever seen one of these unlovable specimens alone. Here on the Barred Os there were dozens of them and an unattractive sight they were too. When Fats introduced him to them, these men welcomed Dan at once as a young fellow after their own delinquent hearts. It irked the young man to be regarded as such a character, but he realized well enough that his safety, indeed his very life, probably depended upon the imposture and so he simply smiled at the others and made himself as agreeable as he could.

Later that day, after most of the work around the ranch had been undertaken, Dan Lewis was given ample proof of the danger in which he stood. The incident erupted from a trifling cause and it was all over before the boy had realized that anything was happening. Here is how it chanced.

At around dusk, four of the men commenced to play draw poker for matchsticks. The men concerned were all well acquainted and tolerably good friends with each other. By ill fortune, an accusation of sharp practice was made by two of the men against one of the others. All four of them were as sober as judges and no money was at stake. You might have thought that the squabble would just fizzle out in a flurry of recriminations, but the fourth member of the group took it into his head to take offence on behalf of the one accused of cheating. It was no affair of his, but he was feeling a mite irritable and thought that he could vent his feelings upon another couple of men by engaging in a little rough and tumble.

The first intimation that the quarrelsome fellow had that things might perhaps be more serious than he had bargained for came when one of the men who had raised the suspicion of cheating at play said, 'Pistols or knives?' Up to that point, it had looked like a routine fight with fists and boots, of a kind that broke out at least once or twice a day among the men who worked for Dave Carson.

'Pistols or knives?' asked the man who had been unwise enough to involve himself in a dispute which didn't concern him. 'Why, we don't need to go so far, I reckon.'

'Yellow, hey?' said the one spoiling for a deadly confrontation. 'You near as damn it called me a liar just now. Pistols or knives?'

Those nearby had stopped talking and doing whatever else they had been engaged in and watched the situation curiously. Dan Lewis was nearby and thought that this was just the sort of big talk which he had heard before. Neither he, nor any of the others present, really believed that anything would come of it. That was before the man who had issued the challenge touching upon knives or guns drew an enormous Bowie knife from its sheath at the back of his belt and launched a murderous attack upon the man facing him.

Jack Tregarth, the fellow who had at first stuck up for the accused, jumped back and fumbled at his belt for the knife he kept there. By all the rules of such *duellos*, his opponent should at this point have waited for the other man to arm himself, but his attacker was evidently not acquainted with the finer points of such fights. Instead of standing there and waiting patiently, he lunged forward, sweeping his blade in a wide arc and cutting Tregarth's throat. Nearby men leaped to their feet, shouting in protest as they were sprayed with arterial blood. Jack Tregarth stood there for a second or two, with a surprised and baffled expression on his face, like he'd just taken a sip of coffee and found it hotter than was comfortable. Then he fell dead, coming to rest with his face half in the fire that had been started to brew coffee.

The sudden and unexpected death of Jack Tregarth was neither the first, nor the most violent, such death to take place at the Barred Os. It was felt that his killer might perhaps have given the dead man a chance to get his own knife out, but nobody felt in the least inclined to broach this subject – at least not within earshot of the man himself. That individual had already made it plain that he took any sort of criticism very ill indeed.

Dan Lewis, although he had been pretty near the murder, had not been one of those to be spattered with blood. Nevertheless, the whole business had a profoundly unsettling effect upon him. The death itself was shocking enough, but it was the attitudes of those around him that Dan found most alarming. They treated the untimely end of Jack Tregarth as a kind of grim joke: just another misfortune, such as could befall anybody. There was clearly going to be no effort to bring home the murder to the perpetrator and even the man who had originally been suspected of sharping did not seem eager to avenge the fellow who had stood up for him. Later that night, two men removed Tregarth's corpse and Dan never heard what had become of it.

Both the Triple C and the South Texas Livestock Company had banded together with others to hire a man from Pinkerton's; somebody who would get to the bottom of the rustling racket that they were sure was operating in that part of the state. Goldman was the man who was being paid by the agency to investigate the business and when he had gathered as much information as he could, it would be his duty to let head office in Chicago know what was going on. It surely was a pity, though, to spend all this time collecting the facts and lying on his belly to spy on a bunch of cowboys and then just draw his usual wage for the job. Even as he was investigating the supposed crime on behalf of

Pinkerton's, Goldman was trying to figure a way of making a little on the side and he thought that he had come up with a surefire way of doing so.

It was reasonably certain that the owners of the Three Cs and the S.T.L.C. would not recognize him as a Pinkerton's man. They would already have paid his boss a retainer. Why not just ride over to the Three Cs and sell them the facts about Dave Carson's little operation? Abe Goldman felt confident of his ability to tinker with his report, so that when Pinkerton's sent it in to the owner of the Triple C, he would not realize that he had already paid for this same information.

Having found out as much as he was likely to do about Carson's scheme, the Pinkerton's agent could see no reason, other than a strictly moral one, why he should not beetle down to the Three Cs and inform the owner of the ranch about all that he had discovered. Most likely, thought Goldman, he wouldn't even need to broach the topic of payment himself: Carmichael would be so grateful, he would shower Abe with gold as a matter of course.

Having made his plans, Goldman wriggled back from his vantage point overlooking the Barred Os and then, when once he was out of sight, he stood up and walked at a brisk pace back to where he had left his horse. There was little enough point in hanging around here any further.

The death of Jack Tregarth cast somewhat of a dampener on the spirits of those working at the

Barred Os. It was not that they were squeamish and delicate men, quite the contrary, but they expected at least some good motive for murder. That one of their fellows had been slain for no other reason than that he had raised an objection to his partner being charged with cheating at play, was a little much, even by their standards. There was no more card play after the death and everybody, as though by common consent, turned in earlier than usual. Nothing was actually said to the hulking creature who had killed Tregarth: after all, nobody had any particular wish to share his fate; but it was plain that in their own rough way, they wanted to indicate their disapproval of his actions.

As he lay in his cot that night, after the lamps had been extinguished, Dan Lewis listened to the desultory conversation in the bunkhouse.

'That's a hell of a thing to happen!'

'Yeah. Still and all, Jack should o' known better than to cross that greaser.'

'You got that right!'

'Mind,' said a third voice in the darkness, 'nobody asked him to go mixing it in that quarrel. He might o' guessed as it would end badly.'

'Happen so,' said the first man who had spoken, 'but I'll warrant he never thought it would be the death of him.'

There was silence for a minute or more. All the men were hunkered down in their cots and the darkness was nigh-on impenetrable in the large room. At length, another man said, 'It says in scripture as getting involved in somebody else's quarrel is as bad as grabbing a strange dog by the ears.'

'Nobody gives a stuff about scripture,' opined the man in the next bed. 'But even so, there's something in what you say. If'n Jack Tregarth had kept his mouth closed when trouble began, then like as not the lightning would have struck the other fellow and passed him by.'

These words were the last observation to be passed on the matter in the bunkhouse in which Dan was sleeping. After a space, the large room fell silent; apart, that is, from the stertorous snuffles and occasional farts that punctuated the stillness.

Even after all the others were sleeping, Dan found that he was still wide awake. After tossing and turning restlessly, he thought that he might as well get up and go for a walk. He climbed out of his bed, pulled on his clothes and picked up his boots – tiptoeing from the room in his stockinged feet, to avoid waking any of the others.

Outside the bunkhouse, the night was moonless and peaceful. It felt good to be in the fresh air. Dan pulled on his boots and thought that as sleep had utterly deserted him, he might just as well take a turn up to the corrals and back. Perhaps the exercise would tire him out a little. He had to step carefully, because it was easy to trip over in the gloom.

The corrals were really more in the nature of

holding pens than anything else. Cattle brought to the Barred Os might typically stay in a fenced field for a few days, before being moved on. There was a natural desire on the part of those working with the steers not to keep them in fenced enclosures for any longer than was necessary. The creatures were always breaking down the wooden fence posts and this meant being roused at any hour of the day or night to help herd them back again and also to repair the broken fences. At that time, the corrals chiefly contained calves.

Two of the calves which Dan had earlier helped to brand came up and nuzzled him, as he stood by the rail. They did not appear to bear him any ill will for his part in pressing red-hot irons against their skin earlier that day. He looked at the marks that he and Fats had left and was pleasantly surprised to find that it was as Fats had said: only the outer layer of skin was blackened. Another calf wandered over and Dan chucked that too behind the ears and craned round in the uncertain light to see how this one was bearing up.

When he peered closely at the brand on the calf's rump, Dan received a sudden shock. Instead of the Barred Os which he expected to see, he found that he was looking at the Three Cs of the Carmichael Cattle Company. Really, this should not have come as any great surprise; after all, he knew that these boys were rustling. It was the sight of that brand, after having just seen the Barred Os, which gave

Dan Lewis the jolt, because he knew at once what was going on and how Carson and his men were working their racket.

CHAPTER 5

Abraham Goldman loathed sleeping rough. Sometimes it was needful, but he detested the experience none the less for that. It was a chilly night, but Goldman didn't want to light a fire. He had no desire to draw attention to his presence out here in the wilds. With luck, he should reach the Carmichael ranch by early evening on the next day and then, after having gained a handsome tip from the Three Cs, he would have to race to the nearest town and telegraph Head Office and prepare his official report. It was likely to be a damned fine balancing act: knowing how much information to reveal to each party, so that he didn't come across as a slippery chancer who was selling the same goods twice.

As Abe Goldman was drifting off to sleep, Dan was standing by the rail of the corral, wondering if he now had everything that he would need to clear his name of the taint of rustling. It would do no harm to take along one or two pieces of hard evidence and so he decided to collect a couple of branding irons the next night, before hightailing it out of the Barred Os. The young man was feeling pretty braced with himself, when he turned to go back to the bunkhouse and found the man who had killed Jack Tregarth standing a few yards away and surveying him with no friendly eye.

'Can I help you?' asked Dan politely. 'Is there something you want?'

'You makin' game of me?' enquired the other, an ugly expression on his face. 'You want to try that again?'

It dawned slowly on Dan that here was a man who had snuffed out the life of another with as little concern as if he had been swatting a fly and that this same fellow was now standing right there in front of Dan, seemingly getting pissed off with him. One grotesque and irrelevant thought flashed through his mind and this was that he hadn't even caught the man's name when the men in the bunkhouse were talking the matter over, that night. How strange, if he were to be killed by somebody whose name he could not even call to mind!

Looking back on the event later, Dan Lewis was never able to work out what prompted the man to attack him. Did he really think that Dan had been mocking him? Was he charged by Dave Carson with keeping an eye on the corrals? Or, and this was the conclusion that Dan favoured in the end, was the man just plain mean and likely to try and kill anybody on the most trifling pretext? Whatever the true explanation, a few seconds after they had spoken, Dan Lewis found himself fighting for his life.

Actually, the whole thing was over so swiftly, that it would hardly be fair to describe it as a 'fight' at all. The hulking fellow came lumbering at Dan, who leaped nimbly to one side. He reached out to steady himself as he jumped out of the way and found that his hand clasped a vertical support, albeit a wobbly one. He recognized by the feel of the thing the T-shaped handle of a spade and as his attacker turned and once more charged towards him, Dan picked up the spade, whirled it around his head and then swung it at the man who was menacing his life.

There was a sharp impact, which jarred all the way up Dan's wrists and arms. He let fall the spade and found that his fingers were stinging with the unexpected shock. Then he recalled his danger and skittered back; out of reach of the crazed man who seemed determined to have his blood. He need not have bothered. The ground trembled beneath Dan's feet as the huge man against whom he had been fighting crashed to the earth like a felled tree.

Picking up the spade, Dan waited for the next attack. It did not come. The man stretched out in front of him lay utterly still and, as far as Dan was able to gauge, was not even breathing. With his heart in his throat, ready at any second to retreat, he bent down to examine the opponent who had, a few seconds earlier, been trying to take his life. Even close up, Dan could not hear the man breathing. He bent closer still, until his ear was practically against the man's chest; still nothing. Then he noticed something which sent a shiver of horror though the whole of his being. The prone man's head was lolling at the most peculiar angle, almost as though it was not properly attached to the neck. Tentatively, hardly knowing what he was doing, Dan reached out his hand and touched the head. He prodded it and almost screamed when it flopped loosely to one side. There could be not the slightest doubt: his wild blow with the spade had broken the fellow's neck.

It was one hell of a thing to find that you had killed a man; especially when you were just a shade over seventeen years of age. Much to his credit, Dan Lewis didn't have hysterics or start sobbing or any foolishness of that kind. Instead, he thought to himself, Well, it was him or me and so I don't see where I had another choice. I seed how he served Jack Tregarth this very night and I don't see that I was under a duty to stand there and let him do the same to me. Still and all, it is a big thing.

It didn't take Dan long to come to terms with what he had done and also to figure out that he'd best not stand there arguing the whys and wherefores of the case to himself. He needed to make tracks and that right speedily. There was no question now of waiting for another day or two, before leaving; he had to get out of there right now, this very minute. As he turned to leave, it struck the boy that it would be a pity not to make any advantage of this incident that he was able. He accordingly reached down and relieved the dead man of his gun, for which he would have no further use in this world. Dan hefted the pistol in his hand, liking the feel of it. He already had the Navy Colt that he had found buried in the mud; this was tucked in the right-hand side of his belt. He popped the new weapon into the left side and then, despite the grimness of his situation, could not help chuckling out loud. He said to the darkness, 'I look like something out of a dime novel. "Two-Guns Lewis" maybe or "The Indian Falls Kid".'

'What do you make of that new fellow, the boy?' asked Dave Carson. He and Fats were sitting at their ease in Carson's house, a substantial, stone-built edifice which in contrast to the nearby bunkhouses was luxuriously appointed. Red velvet curtains covered the windows and no fewer than six lamps cast their mellow light around the room. Things were certainly going all right for some folk, thought Fats to himself; he wouldn't have minded living like this himself.

'Well?' said Carson, a mite impatiently. 'You think he's up to the business?'

'I dare say,' replied Fats cautiously. 'Strikes me as a bit slow, but I'll wager I can cure him of that.'

'We'll need to get some of those critters moving north in the next few days. I don't want you taking them this time. Who else could act as trail boss?'

The man known to one and all as 'Fats' thought this over for a few moments, before saying, 'There's two as would do the job well enough.'

'Send them to me in the morning. Listen, you think it's time to expand a little? Move farther afield?'

Fats stared at his boss in amazement and horror. 'What are you saying?' he asked, when he had recovered himself a little. 'The boot's all on the other foot. We need to be cutting down our activities, not rampin' 'em up. Really, it's not to be thought of.'

Carson looked at his old assistant and said in a surprised tone, 'What ails you, man? You've never been nervous about our business before. Not losing your courage at this late stage, I hope?'

'Courage don't enter into the equation,' said Fats coldly. 'Fact is, we been hitting those drives too hard of late. You know we lost two good men just a day or two back. We need to hold our horses and lay off for a spell. Don't talk to me about courage.'

'Don't take on,' said Carson soothingly, 'I meant nothing by it. But this year is the best yet for the cattle drives and it seems a shame not to take our fair share of the profits.'

After he had left Dave Carson and was prowling

round the ranch, checking that all was in order before he turned in, Fats wondered if his boss was losing his mind. They had been taking more and more chances lately, which was how those two boys had ended up being hanged. From a carefully planned operation, where the number of steers being taken was gauged to a nicety, this whole business was turning rapidly into a free-for-all with every man grabbing as many cattle as he could manage, in the hope of the bonus he would collect from Carson. To Fats's mind, this was a recipe for disaster. Unbridled greed of that kind would be certain-sure to draw the attention of folk to their little racket and that sooner, rather than later. Although he had been working with Carson since the end of the war, Fats wondered if the time had perhaps come to move on and maybe start a little work on his own account. He was under no illusions at all as to the consequences if the two big livestock companies in South Texas found proof of what they had been up to here.

As he neared the corrals where the calves were being kept, Fats stopped and lit the cigar with which his boss had favoured him. The lucifer flared yellow, filling the night with its sulphurous fumes and destroying Fats's night vision. Which was why he actually tripped over the soft obstacle which lay nigh to the rails surrounding the corral and crashed sprawling to the ground. At first, he thought that he had stumbled over the body of a calf. As he got to his feet, cursing, Fats lit another match to see what was what and found himself gazing down at the lifeless body of 'Angel' Garcia – the most feared man on the Barred Os.

'The hell is going on?' muttered Fats to himself. He knelt down to see what had befallen the dead man, by which time the lucifer had burned down and singed his fingers. He lit another and examined the corpse. It didn't take a doctor to see that Garcia's neck had been broken: his head was lolling as loosely as though it had belonged to a rag doll. There was a deep cut in the side of his neck as well.

Tacking up his horse in pitch darkness had not been easy, but Dan knew that lighting a lamp would not have been the smart move. The last thing he wished was to draw attention to himself or invite a heap of questions. It was his ardent wish that he might just slip away from the Barred Os without any fuss or bother. He hoped that nobody would think it worth pursuing him.

Once his horse was ready, the young man led her along the way leading to the open country. There were lights on in the big house, but nobody appeared to be up and about on the ranch itself. With a little luck, thought Dan to himself, I will make some town with a sheriff tomorrow and then my name will be cleared. When you are young, everything often seems very straightforward and clear in this way. Dan Lewis honestly believed that night that his adventures were coming to an end, whereas the reality was that they had hardly begun.

The owner of the Barred Os was mightily surprised and not overly pleased, when his foreman started hammering on the door. Dave Carson had changed into his nightshirt and was preparing to lie in bed for a space, reading Mr Dickens's latest novel. 'I'm coming,' he shouted down the stairs. 'Don't stove in that door, now.'

When he opened the front door, Carson was not delighted to find Fats waiting on the doorstep. 'What is it now?' he asked. 'Surely it could have waited 'til morning?'

'Not hardly!' said the foreman and filled his boss in on what he had found up by the corral.

The two men had brought a lamp up to the corral and were carefully examining the body of the late Angel Garcia. 'What do you make of this cut in his throat?' asked Carson of the other man. 'You think that's what killed him?'

'Wouldn't o' said so, no. See there, his neck's been snapped like a twig. I'd say he died of that.'

'It was enough having him kill Tregarth. I don't want such deaths to become a regular feature here. It's apt to get the law involved soon or late.'

'You want that I should rouse the men?' asked Fats. 'Try to look into it now?'

'You think it was one of my boys who did this?'

'It's what you might call a mighty strange coincidence, that Garcia cuts a man's throat tonight and then a few hours later ends up lying dead with his own throat slashed like that.'

'You're right,' said Carson. 'Wake up the men and let's see if anybody has bloodstains on their clothes or injuries or what have you.'

'A half-dozen men are like to have blood on their clothes. Meaning those as was sitting near Tregarth when he was killed. I tell you now, Garcia was not the most popular fellow around here.'

It didn't take long for Dave Carson and Fats to discover that their newest recruit had gone missing; a very short time after joining them and immediately after the violent and unexplained death of one of their hands. 'There's little enough point in going after him in the dark,' said Fats. 'Why don't we see how things stand in the morning?'

'How things stand?' said Carson. 'How things stand? I can tell you right now how things stand, you clod. How it stands is that this young fellow has come here snooping and now gone haring off to the law to lay an information against us.'

'You think so?'

'It's plain as a pikestaff. He's gulled you into fetching him here, looked round, seen the lie of the land and has gone off now in search of a reward.'

'I still say,' repeated Fats stubbornly, 'as there's no point in going after him now.'

'That at least is true. Let those men sleep now, but at first light, I want half of them riding out and finding that boy. Then I want him questioned, thoroughly, to find out what he was about. Is that clear?'

It was clear enough to Fats and he didn't need to have it spelled out in detail what was to be done with the boy after this 'thorough questioning'. His own acumen and efficiency had been compromised by bringing that young man to the Barred Os and so Fats had a strong personal stake in settling the business neatly and ensuring that Dan Lewis, if indeed that was his real name, did not get a chance to cause any trouble for him and his boss.

Abe Goldman was woken at dawn's early light by a tickling feeling on his nose and a strange hissing sound. He tried to ignore both and go back to sleep, but in the end, he opened his eyes and received the greatest shock he had ever had in the whole course of his life. He found himself staring into the eyes of a coyote, which had been sniffing his face and, by the look of it, getting ready to bite off his nose. Goldman sat up quickly and shouted at the coyote, 'Get on out of it, you damned dirty mongrel!' The dog loped away at once.

This, thought Goldman bitterly, was just exactly the sort of thing which happened when once you left the city and ventured into the open country. If it wasn't coyotes, it would be wolves, bears, Indians and the Lord knew what else. What it must be like for those unfortunate souls who actually lived out here, he simply could not imagine.

After shaking some of the dust and grit from his clothes, it occurred to Goldman that he had not even thought to provide himself with breakfast.

There again, you had the stark difference between town and country. If he had chanced to fall asleep in a civilized spot, say Central park in New York, then all that would be needful if he were hungry would be to hunt out an eating house. Such establishments were to be found on every street corner of the average city. What in the hell did folk do round here when they wanted a bite to eat? Goldman could not for the life of him fathom how anybody could survive under these conditions. Dolefully, he tacked up his horse and rode south; wondering how long it would be before he fainted from hunger.

Others, besides the Pinkerton's agent, were also up bright and early that morning – Dan Lewis for one. He had ridden through the dark for a few hours after leaving the Barred Os, but then stopped to snatch an hour or two of sleep. Young as he was, he had the sense to know that it would be very far from healthy for him to be found within a hundred miles of the Barred Os. He trusted his instincts to awaken him at dawn and planned to start south pretty well immediately.

It was, thought Dan, a glorious day and he only wished that his circumstances were such that he might just amble along slowly and perhaps stop off in some beautiful spot for a picnic meal. As it stood, he needed to move right this minute. Skipping breakfast was no sort of hardship to the boy. Often enough back home, he would set to work for an hour or more upon rising and only later break his fast. He guessed that something would turn up and even if it didn't, well, there were worse things in this world than riding with an empty belly.

Dan Lewis and Abraham Goldman might have been starting out the day without breakfast, but this was not the case for the men at the Barred Os. They were provided with food and coffee before they set out in pursuit of the young man who, it was rumoured, had killed Garcia. However, the cowboys were not allowed the leisure to enjoy their comestibles, because Fats was chivvying them about and trying to speed them up; emphasizing the importance of being on the trail as early as could be.

Truth to tell, most of the nine men who had been selected to hunt down young Dan could not see why this was a desperately urgent task. They understood that he had killed the 'Angel', which was a surprising and, they thought privately, a praiseworthy achievement. Nobody had any great love for the lowering Mexican and when word came that his neck had been broken, there was little grief to be observed. Quite the opposite, in fact, with the men muttering to each other remarks such as, 'Bastard had it coming to him!', 'That's no great loss!' and even harsher judgements upon the matter. Even when Fats tried to impress on them their own danger, by representing that the missing boy might be about to inform on them to the law, there was still little enthusiasm for the pursuit.

'He weren't a bad kid,' said one man. 'I don't think he'd betray us.'

'You stupid cowson,' said Fats angrily. 'You'd take oath on that, would you? If you don't value your own neck, then there's those of us that do our own. You forgetting that this here is a hanging matter?'

'I ain't forgettin' that,' replied the man defensively. 'I'm a-sayin' as that young fellow didn't strike me as the treacherous type. He had a nice, honest face.'

'Yes and you'd know all about honesty, wouldn't you?' said Fats contemptuously. 'When all's said and done, you're an honest type yourself, aren't you, and I don't think! Just get your ass in that saddle and ride him to earth.'

So it was that an hour after sun-up, ten of the roughest and most unprincipled types that you could ever hope to encounter rode out from the Barred Os intending to track down young Dan Lewis and then put an end to his life.

CHAPTER 6

At first sight, all the advantage lay with the men from the Barred Os when it came to the contest between them and Dan Lewis. Had you known nothing about either of the parties, you might have thought that there could hardly have been a more unequal match: ten ruthless and determined grown men, all armed to the teeth on one side, and on the other, a boy of barely seventeen years of age with little experience of the world, other than that gained on his mother's farm. Still and all, things are not always as they first appear and whatever it looked like on the surface, the odds were not really so stacked against young Dan Lewis as at first sight appeared.

For the last three years, Dan had been, in effect, the man of the smallholding which his mother ran. He had been doing a man's work physically since he was fourteen years of age. This had made him as tough and wiry as any grown man and stronger than most. He was used to going on short commons, too; the farm not being so successful as to make his mother and him assured every day of a full stomach.

There was more to Dan Lewis, though, than just being able to put up with a little hardship. He also happened to be the best shot in the county whether the weapon was a scattergun, rifle or pistol. As a child, he had learned that his was an unerring eye with a slingshot; he simply hit what he aimed at and that was all there was to it. When he was twelve, a neighbour had allowed Dan to join him on a hunting expedition. The man had pitied the fatherless child and thought that a day or two away from his home might be a treat for the boy. That trip was a turning point in Dan's life, because it was the first time that he had ever been permitted to handle a firearm.

At first, the farmer had been reluctant to let the boy fire the twelve-gauge scattergun which was almost as long as the boy was tall. Still, he reasoned, what was the worst thing that could happen; maybe a bruised shoulder from the recoil? When Dan took that weapon in his hands, he knew at once that it was nothing more than a cumbersome and exceedingly noisy slingshot. He held it for a moment, saw a duck flying overhead and then, all in one fluid movement, raised it to his shoulder and fired at once. Old Jed was taken aback by the speed of it. He was even more taken aback when the dead duck landed on his head and nearly knocked him senseless.

'Hoo, boy,' said Jed, when he'd picked himself up from the ground. 'That was one lucky shot!'

Dan turned to the old man and said politely, 'Oh no, Mr Carter, that wasn't luck. I meant to hit it.'

'Let me see you do it again. You got a barrel still charged.'

No sooner were the words out of Jed Carter's mouth, than Dan raised the gun once more, and this time let fly at a squirrel on a branch some fifty yards away. Once more, he hit the creature without even appearing to aim. By the time that hunting trip was over, Jed was convinced that the boy was the best shot he'd ever met in his life.

Mrs Lewis wasn't all that amazed when she learned that her son was a regular whizz with a scattergun. Her husband had been a crack shot in the army and she recollected that skills like marksmanship were apparently handed down from father to son. She allowed the boy to take out his father's gun, which she had previously kept locked away, and he soon began providing the two of them with meat for the pot: jackrabbit, squirrels, birds and anything else which crossed his path. This was useful in its own way, but it led to more, and became an occasional source of cash money for Dan and his mother.

For some while, neither Dan nor Mrs Lewis knew if the boy would be as good with a pistol or rifle as he was with his pa's old scattergun. In time, men started dropping round at the farm, to see if young

Dan Lewis was all he was cracked on to be in the shooting line. He was, and visitors soon found that the boy could shoot straighter than any of them.

In the summer, fairs were sometimes held at Indian Falls and other nearby towns, such as the county seat of the area. A popular feature of some of these events were shooting matches with men competing for a cash prize. One day, a man who lived in Indian Falls came to visit Dan and Mrs Lewis with a proposal. He suggested that he should accompany Dan to the county show, lend him a gun and then they would share the prize money if he won.

Mrs Lewis was more than a little dubious when first she heard this notion, but her son was so keen on showing off his prowess in front of a bunch of strangers that she felt it would be unkind to prevent him. The county fair netted a purse of a hundred dollars, which Dan and the owner of the rifle which he used split right down the middle. Over the last few years, Dan had made a fair piece of money from this game.

This, then, was the sort of person that those ten men were hunting: a tough, self-reliant young man who could shoot better than any of them could ever hope to. True, he had never yet shot a man, but then neither had eight of the ten who were tracking him. All things considered, the odds were a lot closer than most folk would have thought.

By about midday, as the group of riders from the

Barred Os were catching up with Dan Lewis, Abraham Goldman had a stroke of luck. He had been budgeting on not getting to the ranch run by the Carmichael Cattle Company until the evening at the very earliest. By good fortune, though, he stumbled upon the founder of that enterprise himself – Ezra Carmichael – in person.

In recent years, Ezra Carmichael had delegated much of the day-to-day running of the Three Cs to his nephew, Jethro. From time to time the old man had a hankering to revisit his youth. This wistful longing took various forms, most of which were familiar to the men working for the Triple C. For instance, one morning they might get up to find that their boss had cooked up breakfast for them. Another day, he would join in the branding – swearing like a mule skinner and expecting them to treat him like just another cowboy. A few days previously, Ezra Carmichael had announced his intention of joining a cattle drive to Elsworth. The large drive, for which Dan Lewis had been engaged, had only left a few days earlier, but there were another five hundred steers which also needed to be taken up to Elsworth. Despite anything that his nephew could say to the contrary, old man Carmichael was determined that he would ride the trail one last time.

'You're sixty-four years of age,' Jethro had reminded his uncle. 'Suppose you take a fall or something?'

'I suppose you'd like to see me snoozing in a

rocking chair or something o' that sort?' replied
Ezra Carmichael testily. 'Well, you needn't think it
for a moment. I built up this business and as long as
I've got breath in my body, I'll carry on working for
it.'

It was hopeless to argue with the old man when
he was in that frame of mind and so Jethro
instructed the trail boss to set an eye on his uncle
and warned him that if any harm befell the old
man, then the trail boss would be looking for
another position that self same day.

So it was that Ezra Carmichael was trotting along
the track leading south towards Indian Falls when
Abe Goldman saw in the distance the column of
dust rising from the cattle drive into the clear
morning sky. An hour later, he could see that it was
indeed a cattle drive and a glance at the brand on
the nearest steer told him whose. It was when he saw
an elderly party, clearly the wrong side of sixty, that
he guessed that this was the very man he was
heading to see. He had heard the stories about Ezra
Carmichael and his endless attempts to rekindle the
passions of his youth.

'Excuse me, sir,' said Goldman courteously, 'but
might I be addressing the proprietor of the
Carmichael Cattle Company?'

'What of it?' replied Carmichael shortly.

'Well, sir, I have some information for you that
you might be glad to hear about.'

'What are you, spy or informer?' asked the old

man shrewdly.

Abe Goldman was a little taken aback by such bluntness. This was not at all how he had rehearsed the interview in his mind. 'I, that is to say, I have to tell you. . . . Well, that is. . . .'

'You got aught to tell me, then you best up and out with it. We got five hundred head o' cattle to get to Elsworth this side of summer. What is it?'

Briefly and without naming the ranch or its owner, Goldman gave an outline of the racket that he had uncovered. As he talked, old Ezra Carmichael's face grew darker and it was plain that he was in the grip of strong emotions. When Goldman had finished, Carmichael said, 'All right, out with it, man. Who's running this rustling game?' When there was no immediate answer, he said slowly, 'Ah, that's the way of it, is it? You want paying first. Well, the choice is yours. I can give you some gold now or if you'd sooner wait for more, I can let you have an IOU. You can redeem it up at my spread, my nephew'll pay out.'

The last thing that Goldman wanted was to start fooling around with names and bits of paper. He was playing a tricky enough game as it was; one which might yet end in his losing his position with Pinkerton's if it should come to light that he had put the bite on a client for extra payment. He said, 'I reckon, sir, as I'll take whatever you happen to have here in cash money.'

The old man stared thoughtfully at Abraham

Goldman. 'You had better not be trying to rob me. I have a long reach in these parts.'

Goldman shivered, as though somebody had just walked over his grave. 'I'm not cheating you, Mr Carmichael. I'll put you on to the man who is stealing so many of your cattle.'

Ezra Carmichael took out a leather bag and counted out ten gold $10 pieces. He handed these to Goldman, saying, 'Let's have that name.'

'It's Carson. David Carson. He owns a spread as lies a few hours south of here.'

'I know the name. Met the man too, if it comes to that. Well, I'm greatly obliged to you, Mister. . . ?'

'Jackson, Joe Jackson.'

'Thank you, Mr Jackson.'

Ezra Carmichael watched as Goldman rode back the way he had come. There goes a crawling snake, if ever I saw one, thought the old man to himself. Once the man was out of earshot, Carmichael called over one of the men and said, 'Ride on and find your trail boss, whatsisname, Lenny. Tell him that I want to see him right this very minute.'

Dan knew that he was being followed and could take a good guess at how far behind him the pursuers were. That these were men from the Barred Os wasn't hard to work out and nor did it take any kind of genius to know that they meant him ill. Dan Lewis was a God-fearing young man and not given to cursing and strong language, but when he looked back and saw that a dozen or so riders were on his tail, he muttered to himself, 'All right, you bastards, let's see you take me.' Strangely enough, he wasn't scared in the least. Sure, he was a mite nervous, but his main emotion was one of anger. He had come pretty close to being hanged and all as a direct consequence of those men and their friends.

The road ahead led past a range of low, rocky hills; scarcely high enough to be dignified with the name of mountains and yet tall and craggy enough to look like such at a distance. Dan recollected this row of craggy bluffs; they had passed them on the way north. He spurred his horse on, into a canter, and headed off the track towards the rocky cliffs. If he couldn't arrange some little surprise for those boys on his tail, well, then, his name wasn't Dan Lewis!

Two miles ahead of them, the figure of the lone rider was little more than a black dot, but Fats was certain in his own mind that this was the boy they were seeking. He called to the others to rein in and then, when they were gathered round him, he said, 'You all listen now to me. Here's how we'll play it. I don't want that boy harmed, leastways not 'til I had a chance to question him. Any man as kills that fellow will be leaving the Barred Os this very day. Is that clear? Take him alive.'

One man was incautious enough to ask why and Fats rounded on him savagely. 'Never you mind the whys of the case, you son of a whore. Just do as I bid you. Is that clear enough for you?' It was, and the ten men rode off towards the rocks and cliffs which lay to the right of the trail.

Young and confident as he was, Dan could see plainly that if he rode against ten or a dozen men, then he wasn't likely to come out ahead of the game. As he headed up the slope into the rocky bluff, he scanned the crags carefully, looking for a good location. It didn't take him long to find what seemed to him ideal for his purposes. He had deliberately slowed down to a steady trot, in order to make sure that those following him could see just precisely where he was going. He wanted to know where those men were going to be in fifteen minutes or so. The horse refused to carry him up the smooth, steeply inclined limestone slope and so Dan dismounted and led her up. The mare's hoofs could not get a good purchase on the slick rock and towards the top, Dan felt as though he were dragging the beast up by main force.

Somehow, Dan got both himself and his horse up to the top of the slope, which was littered with boulders and rocks which the frost and rain had split off from the cliffs towering above this vantage point. As he had hoped, there was a way down on the other side: a hair-raisingly steep and precipitous path, which led to a somewhat lower point. He would have to hope and pray that this was not a dead end and that he would be able to get back to the track leading north.

Leaving his horse, Dan crept back to the pile of boulders and scree which lay tumbled everywhere. The rocks varied greatly in size; some were as big as half a house, others no bigger than loaves of bread. The young man hunted around for one of a reasonable size and eventually settled upon a fairly smooth chunk, which came up to his chest and had weathered away until it looked for all the world like a giant pebble. Dan pushed against this tentatively and found that it rocked easily enough. If he put all his strength into the task, he was sure he could tip the thing over and send it rolling down the slope.

'Hold up,' cried Fats, as the band of riders progressed gingerly across the flat expanse of limestone. 'We can't follow a trail cross bare rock. Time to use our brains.'

'He might've gone ahead, round the side, up those slopes or 'most anywhere,' said one of the other men. 'Happen we should split up.' As he finished speaking, there was a faint creaking noise, which rapidly became a rumbling. It was not possible at first to tell where the sound was coming from, because the echoes bounced wildly off the surrounding rock-faces. By the time they knew for sure what was happening there was little enough that could be done about it.

The enormous rock gathered speed as it rolled down the slope towards the riders. A couple of the sharper-witted among them spurred on their mounts frantically to escape, but their horses' hoofs slipped and slid across the slick, white limestone. The other men were paralyzed by surprise and in that attitude two of them were struck by the boulder. One horse was hit side-on, the huge rock shattering the leg of the rider. It was then deflected into another horse, which had its front legs broken. The rider of this horse fell heavily to the ground, fracturing his right arm in the process. Then the next boulder came rattling down the rock slope in their direction.

The angles were such that Dan Lewis was pretty sure that he couldn't be seen from below, as he heaved the rocks down. Nevertheless, he took care to keep low. After setting five of the biggest he could manage rolling on their way, Dan ran off to where his horse was waiting for him. That wasn't a whole heap more difficult than playing skittles, he thought to himself. He mounted up and then, very slowly, urged on his horse down the narrow path leading, he hoped, to the plain below.

The damage inflicted by the rocks which Dan Lewis had sent down on to the ten riders was something else again. The boy had moved fast, setting one boulder after another rolling, and not stopping to see the consequences of his actions. Getting the horses to move quickly on that slippery rock was impossible and the screams of the first injured animals served to spook the others, making them jittery and hard to control. Fats shouted angrily at his men, urging them to stay calm and not try to gallop over such a treacherous surface; but it was all to no avail. It was, as Dan Lewis had thought, just like a game of skittles.

After the fifth rock had come to rest and it looked as though there weren't any more coming, Fats took stock of the situation. It was an absolute disaster. Five of the horses were crippled and they were lying down, whinnying pitifully. Five of his men were similarly out of action, with two of them looking to Fats as if they were like to die. The second man to have been injured, the one who had fallen from his horse and broken his arm, had been struck fairly and squarely by the next rock to come tumbling down. It had split open his head and although he was still breathing, he was quite unconscious. Another fellow's chest had been crushed when his horse fell on to him. The other three wounded men would probably be all right if they received medical attention, although one would perhaps lose his leg.

A terrible, killing rage had engulfed Fats. Everything had been going so well and he still couldn't work out how things had gone so wrong, so quickly. He said to the four men who were still in good shape, 'You men go back on our tracks and then see if you can find him on the other side of that bluff. I'll take oath he's doubled round there. I'm going up yon hill after him.'

'You want one of us should come with you?'

'The kid ain't yet begun to shave. You think I can't brace him by my own self? Just do as you're bid.'

CHAPTER 7

As he trotted along the trail north, Abe Goldman was feeling pretty pleased with himself. He had a handsome tip in his pocket, his time was being paid for by Pinkerton's and he was still alive and breathing. It was a glorious day into the bargain. He wasn't, in general, one for admiring nature and appreciating the great outdoors, but even the most inveterate city dweller could not have failed to notice how grand the world was looking out in the wilds that day.

Goldman's pleasure in the simple joys of the blue sky and fluffy white clouds which scudded across it did not last long. He had been struck by an idea and was cursing himself for a fool for not having considered this new scheme before. Why, he had been throwing money away, hand over fist! He was quite accustomed to selling his goods twice, once to the man paying his salary and often enough to the fellow who was most affected by the information which he had gathered. He had just a few hours earlier pulled this familiar stunt. But why should he stop there? Surely, the owner of the Barred Os might also pay to be warned of the impending arrival of a lynch mob at his ranch?

Mind, it would be a delicate business, extracting the cash without giving too much away in advance. After all, if he simply told Dave Carson that a bunch of angry cattle ranchers were heading his way, then he would have given the man all the information he needed and would be unlikely to earn a cent. On the other hand, he couldn't see any shrewd businessman like Carson handing over money for a pig in a poke. He would have to let the man know that he knew all about his racket and could tip him the wink about some unspecified threat now facing him. It would need careful handling, because if he weren't careful, he might come across in the character of a blackmailer trying to put the bite on somebody. He wouldn't want anybody starting to play rough.

Dan moved as fast as he dared along the narrow path which led down from the bluff. He was expecting at any moment to catch a bullet in his back. It was a fair bet that those men he had used for skittles would be feeling a mite ticked off with him and were all too liable to shoot him without warning.

The way was too steep and the footing too uncertain

91

for him to ride and so the boy was compelled to lead his horse along at an agonizingly slow pace. At last, he turned a sharp bend and was relieved to find that they were almost at the foot of the hill. All that remained was to thread a way through a pile of broken rock and small boulders and they would be back on level ground. It was when he reached the heaps of scree that he saw three riders cantering towards him.

Four men had been directed by Fats to circle round the bluff and try to intercept the young man, if he was hoping to slip down and escape from the other side of the hill. As they left to follow their instructions, one of them, a man called Clinton Rodders, said, 'I signed up to handle steers, not fight some private war.'

'You yellow?' asked one of his companions.

'Call it what you want,' said the other, with a shrug. 'This here's getting too hot for me. I'm off.'

Having said which and without any further ado, Rodders spurred on his horse and vanished at speed.

'Yellow-bellied bastard!' said one of the remaining three, 'You boys ain't affeared to tackle a boy not long out o' diapers?'

It seemed that the three of them were not at all averse to the task in hand and so they set off, veering left around the shoulder of the bluff, until they saw Dan Lewis leading his mount down the rocky incline.

Young as he was, and despite being a pretty good shot, Dan knew better than to ride openly against three opponents simultaneously. Instead, he positioned himself behind the pile of rocks and watched, with some little apprehension, as the riders came on. When they were fifty yards away, he called out, 'That'll be just about close enough.' He hoped that his voice didn't sound as young and nervous to their ears as it did to his.

The three men reined in and one of them shouted, 'You come out o' there with your hands up, son. We don't mean you no harm. Just want to ask you a few questions.'

'I don't think so,' called back Dan. 'I'm setting here, minding my own business. You all leave me be now.'

'Can't do that, boy,' said another of the men. 'We got our orders. Gotta take you to speak a little with our boss and after that I make no doubt you'll be free to go on your way.'

I don't think so, thought Dan wryly, those boys mean me ill or I'm a Dutchman. Still and all, it's a fearful thing to shoot at a fellow being. I surely hope it don't come to any such thing. Despite this, he drew one of the pistols he carried and cocked it with his thumb. He had never in his life even pointed a gun at anybody, let alone pulled the trigger, but he certainly didn't aim to allow himself to be disarmed by those fellows and then carried off to the Lord knew where.

As the three men were engaging him in conversation, they were gradually edging forward, while at the same time moving apart from each other. It needed no great grasp of military strategy to see that the aim was to ouflank him, with two moving in from either side of his position. Dan yelled out, 'That's close enough, you hear me?'

'Come on, son, you don't want any fightin', no more than we do.' And still they were urging on their mounts at a slow walk.

He had no desire at all to start a gun battle, but it was clear enough to Dan that these fellows were not about to back off, leastways not unless he took some decisive action. He fired a single shot, well above their heads. The result was a fusillade of fire aimed seemingly straight at him. Maybe the men had forgotten that they had been instructed not to kill the boy or perhaps they were annoyed at being shot at in that way, but the half-dozen shots loosed off were far too close to be mere warnings. These men were shooting to kill. The final ball loosed in the volley of shots struck a rock, no more than three feet from where Dan was crouching. A splinter of stone flew off and hit his cheek. Dan reached up his hand and felt the blood which was now running down his face. 'That could o' taken out my eye!' he muttered and it was at that moment that he knew he had to act. He hesitated for a second, the significance of killing a man being greatly on his mind. But then he recalled the hangings that he had witnessed and

94

thought of how close he had come to sharing the fate of those men. This hardened his heart and he drew down on the man to the right of the little group, squeezed off a single shot at him and had the satisfaction of seeing the fellow throw up his arms and then fall from the saddle.

For many men, that first time that they kill another human being is a shocking and awe-inspiring event. For Dan Lewis, though, who knew well enough now that he was fighting for his very life, the moment passed all but unnoticed. He knew that unless he was fast about it, his life was like to be sacrificed in the next minute or so.

'Son of a bitch!' said one of the two surviving men. 'The boy done killed Corky. Son of a bitch!' He raised his own pistol again, staring at the rocks to see if he could catch a glimpse of movement. It was a fruitless endeavour, because Dan was already aiming at him and when he saw the man raising his pistol, that was all the encouragement that the young man required. He shot down the second of the men and then, almost without hesitating, he fired at the last man, killing him too.

He was just coming to terms with the fact that he had killed three men with three shots, when Dan heard behind his right ear the unmistakeable metallic click of a pistol being cocked. The man holding the gun said, 'You let that pistol fall, or before God I'm a-goin' to blow out your brains.'

*

Dave Carson was feeling uneasy in his mind. On the face of it, everything was going just fine and dandy for him, with more cattle coming into his control than ever before. He was reaping all the rewards of a big rancher with hardly any of the expense and inconvenience which usually attended such a role. In another year or so, he might be able to think about retiring from the business entirely and living the life of a respectable citizen in some big town. Men had died at the Barred Os before and there was no cause for Garcia's death to affect him greatly. Nevertheless, he had a sense of dread about this death; as though it were a harbinger of doom. Who was that young fellow that he had offered a job to without knowing a damned thing about him? It was in this frame of mind that Abe Goldman encountered the owner of the Barred Os that day.

Carson didn't care for the look of the neat little man who rode up that afternoon. He was alone in the garden at the front of his house, tending to the roses which were his special delight, when he looked up and saw a rider drawing near. When the man was within hailing-distance, Carson called to him, 'Whatever it is, we don't want any today. Or have you got an appointment?'

This sarcasm was altogether lost on Goldman, who responded pleasantly, 'Well, I guess that's a specimen of the thanks you are apt to receive when trying to do a fellow man a good turn. No matter, I'll wish you a very good day, sir.' He turned slowly, as though to leave. Dave Carson couldn't, as the crafty Pinkerton's agent knew very well would be the case, resist asking:

'What is this good turn you wish to do me? You don't look like any sort of philanthropist.'

'Appearances can be terrible deceptive, or so they say. You never read in scripture where many a one has entertained angels unawares?'

Carson gave the visitor an odd look. He said, 'Speaking in general, I am not much of a one for scripture. Not to mention that you do not look a whole lot like an angel, either. Have you come here to talk about the Bible, like some preacher or Sunday School teacher, or is your business of a more practical nature?'

'If it comes to the matter of that,' said Goldman, 'I ain't all that hot on scripture and suchlike myself. Just making conversation and being agreeable.'

'Let's cut out all the nonsense. Suppose you just tell me what you're after?'

Goldman cut out the nonsense, saying, 'You been running a big rustling operation. There are those as are on to you and you're in danger. Give me two hundred dollars and I'll give you chapter and verse of who's after you and why.'

'You talking about the law?'

'I'm saying nary another word, not 'til I got that money in my hand.'

If Abe Goldman had turned up at the Barred Os a day or two earlier, he would have got short shrift with this line, but Carson was already feeling spooked by Garcia's death and the way that young man had dug up immediately afterwards. Hearing that he was in danger simply confirmed what he already knew in his waters. He looked hard at Goldman and then said, 'Wait here.'

It was all that Goldman could do, not to turn round his horse and gallop away from there, when Dave Carson left him and went into the big house. Suppose he came back with a scattergun? That was the way some men would play it, when faced with an attempt to extort money in this way. Although it was a mild afternoon, Goldman was suddenly chilly and rubbed his hands together nervously to try and warm them up.

After five minutes, by which time Abe Goldman's nerves were shredded all to pieces, the owner of the Barred Os came back. In his hand was a little leather bag. He weighed this in his hand and said, 'There's two hundred dollars in cash money in this bag. I'm going to hand it to you, so that you can check it for yourself. Then you tell me what you know.'

He leaned down from his horse and reached out an eager hand, but if Goldman thought he was dealing with a sucker, he was soon disabused of the notion. In a voice soft with menace, Carson said in a matter-of-fact and quiet way, 'If this is some species of trick to part me from my money, then I strongly recommend you to think twice before taking this money. If I find out that you're pulling a stroke on me, I'll call up a few of my men and we'll hunt you down and kill you before you get the chance to spend a dime of this money. That clear enough?'

'It's clear. There's no trickery in the case.'

'You better hope that's true for your own sake.' He handed the bag to the man on the horse, who told him:

'Ezekiel Carmichael knows that you've been preying on his cattle. He's mad as a hornet and heading up here to do you harm. It might take him a day or so to raise a bunch of men, but when he's done so, he'll be after lynching you.'

'How'd you know this? When did Carmichael find this out about me?'

'Oh, not so long since,' said Goldman vaguely. 'Least you can get ready for him.' Now that he had the money, he was anxious to be gone. There was something about Carson's manner that was unsettling. 'Well, our business is done. Reckon I'll be making tracks.' He began to turn the horse.

'Wait up a minute,' said Dave Carson affably, 'I got something here that you might want to see.'

'Hey? What's that?'

Carson put his hand into his jacket pocket and took out a shiny, silver muff pistol; the kind of weapon favoured by gamblers and ladies. He pointed this at Goldman's face. So confident had he been about this new scheme, that the Pinkerton's agent simply could not make sense of this development. He stared stupidly at the derringer, as though he had never seen such a thing before in his life. Then he said, 'I don't know what you're. . . .' He had no chance to complete this sentence, because Dave Carson shot him in the face at a range of less than six feet. The ball took Goldman through his left eye, bored through his brain and then exited from the back of his head in a welter of blood, bone and brain tissue. His horse took fright and reared, before bolting off with the dead man still mounted in the saddle.

Fats had been compelled to leave his horse at the top of the ridge. The boy had, as he had guessed, made his way down from the bluff and he hoped that the other four would be in time to catch him and prevent his escape. His horse could not be persuaded to go down the little track along which Lewis had evidently gone. When he was halfway down the path and could see the plain spread before him like a diorama display, Fats saw three of the men he had sent in pursuit of the boy. They were riding up to the base of the cliff. He couldn't see from this angle, but guessed that Dan Lewis was down there with his horse. Well, he could forget that. Those men would be sure to lay hands on him so that Fats could have a leisurely session of question and answer with him.

When he turned a sharp angle in the path down, Fats could see the boy crouched below him hiding behind a pile of rocks. He heard an exchange of words, but was not close enough to hear clearly what was said. As he speeded up, the shooting began. Fats's main fear was that those damned fools might kill the kid, in flat defiance of his instructions. By the time he was right down at the bottom, the first flurry of shots had ceased and Fats found that he was behind the rocks and could see Dan Lewis ahead of him. The youngster was so preoccupied with the riders bearing down on him that he had not heard Fats approaching from his rear.

As Fats tippy-toed up behind the young man, his aim always being to take the boy alive, he watched in amazement as the three riders were all mercilessly gunned down by a young fellow who scarcely looked old enough to be shaving yet. The gunfire masked the sound of Fats's footsteps and as the echoes of the last shot faded away, he was right behind Dan Lewis with his pistol in his hand.

'You let that pistol fall, or before God I'm a-goin' to blow out your brains.'

Dan knew that the other man had the drop on him and had no especial reason for doubting that the man behind him meant just what he said. He opened his fingers and allowed the Colt Navy to drop to the ground. The man said, 'Now you stand up, real slow and let me see what else you got about you.'

Without making any move which might have

been open to misinterpretation, Dan Lewis got to his feet and stood there waiting further instructions. 'All right, you can turn around now, but keep it slow as you like, on account of I'm already a-squeezin' o' this here trigger and we don't neither of us want any mishaps.'

Carefully, keeping his hands in plain view the whiles, Dan turned to face the man and was not overly surprised to find that it was Fats. He nodded and said, 'Afternoon there.'

'Just reach that other pistol out, with your left hand, and let it fall.' Dan did so. Fats said, 'You done killed five o' my men, you know that? There's three more out of action, one o' them like to lose his leg. You kill Angel as well?'

'I don't recall the name.'

'Boy, you really are something else again,' said Fats, half admiringly, 'I truly never saw the like. It pains me as you ain't on my side. What a one you would o' been to have riding next to me.' Before he had finished speaking, Fats drew back his arm and without any warning, slammed the pistol in his hand against the side of Dan Lewis's head. The two-pound chunk of steel was enough to lay any man out and Dan dropped like a poleaxed ox. The other man followed up this blow with a hefty kick to the youth's ribs and then bent down and delivered another blow to the head, which had the effect of knocking out the young man entirely.

After picking up the boy's two pistols and slapping

him round the face a couple of times to see if he was really out cold, Fats went back up the path at a brisk pace to retrieve his horse. He didn't bother trying again to urge her down the precipitous track, but instead led her back down to where the wounded men were lying, groaning and swearing. Fats told them, 'I'm a-goin' now for help. You men hang on in there and grit your teeth. You ain't none o' you in any fit state to be ridin' your horses. I'll fix up for a cart to come and collect you.' Ignoring the cries for water and pleas not to be left there, he saddled up and walked his horse down from the limestone floor of the little valley and back out into the open country again.

Once he was back on ordinary ground, Fats spurred on his horse into a canter and rode to his left, skirting the bluff, until he came to where he had left the young man. To his relief, he saw that the boy had not stirred. Fats dismounted and ferreted about in his saddle-bag, until he found what he was looking for: a long, rawhide bootlace. Then he went over to Dan, turned the boy over on to his belly and wrenched his arms up behind his back.

The Comanche have a way of immobilizing prisoners which requires no more than a foot-long strip of rawhide. The method is simplicity itself. You force a man's hands behind his back and lash his thumbs together tightly. Then, you pull his two feet back hard and tuck them behind the bound thumbs. A man trussed up in this way will be unable to stand up or indeed do much except for wriggle about uncomfortably. Having ridden with a band of Comancheros for some time, this was the kind of useful tip which Fats had picked up. He tied Dan's thumbs tightly together and then set to waking the boy up. He splashed water from his canteen in Dan's face and then lit a lucifer and pressed it against the bare skin of the young man's neck. That did the trick.

'What's going on?' asked Dan.

'What's going on is that you and me are takin' a little ride. Back to the Barred Os, so's you can explain one or two things to my boss.'

Originally, the plan had been for Fats and his boys to catch up with this young scoundrel in the middle of nowhere and then question him at length, before disposing of him once for all. But after having half his men killed and the others crippled by this one youth, Fats felt a certain reluctance at returning to the Barred Os with a story of abject failure. Let the boss take out his anger on this fellow; let Lewis explain what had been going on and what he was up to. Carson had an uncertain temper and providing a lightning conductor like this, in the form of a person who could be beaten or killed, was, to Fats's way of thinking, a prudent precaution. He didn't want Dave Carson's wrath descending upon his own head alone.

Getting a man with his hands tied behind his

back on to a horse takes a bit of doing, but eventually Fats accomplished the task. Then, they set off north at a sedate walk.

CHAPTER 8

About half a mile down the trail Dan Lewis tumbled from his horse, landing painfully on his face. His nose began to bleed freely. Having his hands secured behind his back in that way might make it all but impossible for him to escape, but it also meant that the two of them could not progress at any rate faster than a walk. Even trotting was out of the question when a man cannot hold the reins. It came as no surprise really when the boy took a fall.

'At least tie my hands in front of me,' said Dan, after Fats had helped him to his feet. 'I'm not fixing to flee and at this rate we'll take better than a week to get back to your ranch.'

'Not a bit of it. There's more to you than meets the eye. I ain't about to free your hands, not for a second. Slow and steady is how we'll make it to the Barred Os.'

As it happened, Fats was quite wrong about this,

because long before they made it to the Barred Os, there was an interruption to their journey which changed everything.

In those first few years after the war, a number of young men found that they couldn't settle to anything in particular and took to drifting across the country – making a living in any way that presented itself. These types worked as cowboys, barkeeps, bounty hunters, lawmen and anything else that turned up. As long as it did not entail staying in one place for too long, they would do just about anything to make ends meet, including highway robbery, which they preferred not to call by its real name, but described rather as, 'working as road agents'. Three such men were working their way through Texas and by chance had staked out a spot along the track where Fats was taking his prisoner.

The road north curved round the edge of another towering monolith, similar to that which was the scene of the recent slaughter in which Fats and Dan had both played a part. In a cave up in the cliff-side, a group of former Confederate soldiers had made their temporary home. At least the cave had the advantage of being warm and dry, which was more than could be said for some of the places where the three men had spent nights in recent months. They had been compelled to flee precipitately from Arkansas leaving that state just one step ahead of a necktie party, composed of citizens who had had just about enough of their depredations.

The first Fats and Dan Lewis knew of all this was when two riders came heading along the track towards them. The two young men looked amiable enough and smiled cheerfully at them. One of them observed, 'It surely is a fine day. A good day to be alive on, wouldn't you say?' Fats grunted an inaudible answer and made to continue on his way. He glanced at Dan, to make sure that there was no effort on the boy's part to take advantage of this chance encounter.

'Mind,' continued the man, 'when I say as it's a good day to be alive on, that is as much as to intimate to the two of you that it would be a shame if you was to die on such a glorious, sunny afternoon.'

'You say what?' said Fats, catching the drift and being none too pleased with what he was hearing. 'That supposed to be a threat?'

'You might put it so,' admitted the young man, raising a sawn-off scattergun which he had previously concealed from sight on the other side of his saddle. 'You go for your gun now, I'm likely to cut you in half with this thing.'

The other rider joined in at this point, drawing a pistol and saying, 'This here is what you might term a hold-up. So you fellows just set right where you are and I'm going to come over and take any guns as you might have hid about your person.'

'Come nigh to me,' said Fats, 'and I'm like to blow your head off.'

'Wouldn't exactly recommend that course of

action. Our friend's up on the bluff there and he's a devil with that rifle of his. Between the three of us, you'd be dead for certain-sure, 'fore you even got that gun clear o' the holster.'

It has to be said that the three robbers had set out the case as clearly as you could wish for and if Fats hadn't been so irritable about losing his followers to a green boy, then he might have proceeded a little more cautiously. Howsoever, his patience was all wore away and he was in no mood for having anybody telling him what he could and could not do. All of which explains why, instead of doing the sensible thing and throwing up his hands, Fats decided rather to go for his gun. Maybe he hadn't set any store by the mention of a rifleman up in the rocks, but it was this man who settled the matter swiftly once and for all.

That was a good shot. The fellow up above them had been a sharpshooter during the war and although his target was a good two hundred yards away, he took out Fats cleanly with a minie ball straight through his head. Dan saw his captor's head explode in a spray of blood, a second before the crack of the rifle reached him. As soon as their friend had fired, the other two men drew down on Dan and one of them said, 'You best bring both your hands into view right now, pilgrim. Otherwise, you're like to go down the same road as your late partner.'

'He weren't my partner,' said Dan, 'and I can't

bring my hands out to show you. They're bound behind me.'

'The hell they are! What's the game? You his prisoner or what?'

'In a manner o' speaking. You going to shoot me or what?'

The fellow holding the scattergun said to his companion, 'Go round and see if he's telling the truth. Keep out o' my line of fire, though.' Then he said to Dan, 'You so much as twitch a muscle and I'm going to blast you straight to hell. That understood?'

'I reckon,' replied Dan laconically.

It took no time at all for the men to discover that Dan was telling no more than the literal truth and the man who saw the thong lashing Dan's thumbs together drew a knife and freed him. After checking that he was unarmed, they allowed him to dismount and stretch his aching muscles. At this point, the man who had killed Fats came ambling down from the cliff and asked his friends what the Sam Hill was going on. Dan explained briefly how he had come to be in such a predicament and the three bandits listened with great interest. At the end of his tale, one of them said, 'So you're a straight type who got caught up in a load of villainy against your wishes. Is that what you'd have us believe?'

'Don't much care if you believe it or not,' said Dan. 'That's what happened.'

'Sounds like the truth,' said another of the men.

'You want to make up a story, you'd make it more likely than that. 'Sides which, look at him. He's only a kid.'

Dan turned a cold eye on the speaker, saying, 'I may only be a kid, but I just lately killed me a half-dozen men.'

'That's nothing to the purpose,' said the third man gruffly. 'We all of us killed men at around the age you are now. You hungry?'

'Yes, sir, I ain't ate nothing today.'

'Never mind the "sir". My name's Brett and this here is Jack and Pete. You bring your mount up away from the road. No percentage in advertising our presence to every passing traveller.'

The others took charge of Fats's horse, which still bore its ghastly burden, leaving Dan to lead his own horse up into the hill and out of view of the road. The three men had established a cosy little camp in a natural depression like a miniature amphitheatre. The cave in which they slept was on one side of this hollow.

There wasn't a whole heap of food, just some cold meat and cornpone, but Dan fell to ravenously. Seldom had he had a better appetite. While he ate, he answered questions from the men, who seemed genuinely interested in his story. While he was eating, the man called Brett brewed up a pot of coffee. As they sipped it, Pete said, 'What are your plans now, youngster?'

'I guess that's up to you men. I don't know how I

stand. You might be a going to shoot me, so's I don't inform on you.'

'Ah, hell, you ain't the treacherous brand,' said Pete. 'Anybody can see that. And we ain't about to shoot a man as we've invited to dinner!'

'You mean I'm free to go?'

'Maybe. If you want to.'

'Meaning?'

'Meaning we might ask if you want to stay.'

'What, and join up with you men?'

'Could be,' said Pete. 'What would you say?'

'It's real kind of you,' began Dan conventionally, before all three of the men burst into laughter. 'What's funny?'

'We ain't kind, not no-how. You strike us as being a handy one with guns. If you've told us no lies?'

'I told you only God's honest truth.'

'So we all thought. What do'you say?'

'Don't take it wrong, but I couldn't steal for a living. It's not how I was raised. I wouldn't sleep easy. All I want is to get things straight and then head back to Indian Falls. Where I live, you know.'

'Well,' said Pete, 'that's a straight answer. I didn't think you was the outlaw type, but we're always glad of a good shot in our line of work, if you follow my meaning.'

'I reckon that I'd as soon find a sheriff and take him over to the Barred Os, if it's all the same to you fellows. Not but that I'm grateful for the offer.'

'I reckon that we can't send you off on foot. It's a

damned nuisance, but I suppose we'd best let you take your horse. That fellow as we killed, you'll maybe be wanting his gun?'

'Any gun'll do.'

'You can take your pick. I dare say we can spare you one of 'em.'

Despite the fact that all three of them were clearly thieves, Dan found the company of Brett, Jack and Pete strangely comforting. When they parted, he enquired as to the whereabouts of the nearest town and was somewhat taken aback to learn that he had been heading in quite the wrong direction. Brett said, 'There's a town, few miles north of here. This drovers' road don't pass through it, though, you need to veer off east. You keep your eyes open, you'll like as not see a little track leading off that direction, maybe fifteen, twenty miles north.'

As he set off again, Dan reflected that he was fit and well, had a full belly, a horse between his legs and a gun at his hip. Everything considered, things could be a whole lot worse.

The messenger that Ezra Carmichael had dispatched to the Triple C arrived late that night. His summons was urgent and plans were made for a body of twenty men to leave at dawn the next day. Like other outfits in Texas, the Three Cs had been growing increasingly concerned about the rustling which was of course why, along with others, they had engaged Pinkerton's to look into the matter. There could be little doubt as to the intentions of this expedition, because they made a point of packing several lengths of stout rope. There was likely to be only one end for whoever was behind the thefts of livestock which had plagued them for the last three years or more.

At about the time that men were being mustered at the Three Cs, Dan Lewis was settling down for a good night's sleep. He was feeling bruised and sore all over, but as far as he could see, he was now within reach of his goal. As he read the case, it was just a question now of handing the business over to a duly appointed peace officer and then he could forget all about it and head back home. With which comforting thought, he fell into a deep and dreamless sleep.

Dave Carson was not a happy man. For one thing, Fats had vanished earlier that day with nine of his best men and he'd heard neither hide nor hair of them since. How long did it take to run to earth a snot-nosed kid and ask him a few questions? Carson was beginning to think that Fats wasn't up to the job any more. If ever there was a time when he needed a good man at his side, that time was right now.

The two men that he instructed to carry Goldman's corpse off and pitch it into a shallow grave well away from the house did not blink at the task; although they caught each other's eyes, when Carson wasn't looking. It was, after all, the third

114

dead body to have been seen on the Barred Os in less than twenty-four hours. One death to be concealed was not uncommon. Two was out of the ordinary and three deaths in this way was frankly alarming. In the bunkhouse, the men were talking in quiet voices about what could be happening. The fact that Fats and a bunch of other men had ridden out that morning and not been seen since had not escaped notice either.

Searching Goldman's belongings had turned up the card identifying him as a Pinkerton's agent which lent verisimilitude to his warnings about the lynch mob heading this way. That evening, the owner of the Barred Os had set his men to covering up all traces of illegal activity. A few mavericks had been hastily branded and one or two steers with the markings of either the Carmichael Cattle Company or the South Texas Livestock Company had been slaughtered and butchered – the telltale pieces of skin bearing the brands having been burnt. As far as Carson could see, there was no actual evidence of wrongdoing about the place. Not that this was altogether relevant in an affair of this sort. Whoever fetched up here was not going to be conducting a regular court case with witnesses, statements on oath and a judge presiding over it all. The suspicion alone would be grounds for a hanging. Especially after whatever that sneaky little Pinkerton's man might have told them. Had he been watching this place? It was entirely possible.

As he mulled things over, Carson was considering what use he might be able to make of what he sometimes thought of as his ace in the hole. This was the fact that the sheriff in Oxbow, the nearest town, was, as the saying went, in his pocket.

The previous man to hold the post of sheriff had been a right awkward cowson: always sniffing around and looking for trouble. He'd had his own ideas about Carson and his little operation, that was for sure. Still, it had never progressed as far as an arrest, let alone any sort of trial. The new man, though, who had been appointed eighteen months ago, was a horse of a different colour. Soon after he took on the job, he came by Carson's place with a sheaf of papers which he said he had unearthed when clearing out his predecessor's desk. They were the notes that the old sheriff had made of his investigations into rustling. It had been a cold fall day and a cheerful fire had been blazing in Carson's study, where he had invited the sheriff when he came calling. The man had told Carson what these papers were and then, very casually, he had walked over to the fireplace and tossed them into the flames. Before Sheriff Fuller had left the Barred Os, Carson had begged him to accept a donation for whatever charitable concern was dearest to the sheriff's heart in Oxbow. They had understood each other very well.

From that day since, Fuller had come by Carson's place once a month and after exchanging pleasantries in the study and sharing a glass of good liquor, Carson had handed over a sum of cash; both of the men still maintaining the fiction that this was to be forwarded to some charity or other. A year and a half later, Carson still couldn't work out whether he was bribing the sheriff or was himself being blackmailed by that official. Not that it made much odds; the important thing was that Sheriff Fuller seemed willing and able to keep trouble away from Carson's door, in exchange for a regular bundle of cash money.

The question now confronting Carson was if he should ride over to Oxbow and tell the sheriff what was going on and try to enlist his aid. How far would Fuller be prepared to stretch out his neck and hazard his own position? Not very far at all, would have been Dave Carson's guess. That being so, it probably made more sense for him to make his own arrangements here and leave Fuller out of the reckoning. He surely wished that Fats would hurry up and get back with that posse of men, because Carson had an idea that he was going to need all the guns he could muster in the coming days.

Oxbow was a pretty little town, where nothing much ever seemed to happen. Its collection of little white-painted clapboard houses looked as though it would be more at home in New England than in southern Texas. Although it lay only a few miles from the Chisholm Trail, there was no reason for the cattle drives to impinge upon the serenity of Oxbow. The cowboys and their steers who passed five miles to the west were in too much of a hurry to reach Elsworth and Abilene for them to stop off at Oxbow to make whoopee.

Gaining the post of sheriff of this quiet town had been something of a coup for Gerry Fuller. He'd had to grease one or two palms and menace one member of the town council, but now he was securely in the saddle and that was where he meant to stay.

None of which was known by Dan Lewis when he rode into Oxbow that morning. All he saw was a nice, respectable-looking town, similar in some ways to Indian Falls apart of course from the idiosyncratic architecture. He was sure that once he had set the situation out before the sheriff, it would simply be a question of waiting for a day or two until the man running the rustling operation was arrested and his own name cleared.

Fuller was sitting behind his desk in the front office when the street door opened and a very young fellow walked in off the sidewalk. The boy was probably no more than ten years younger than Fuller himself, but he had the look of a real Rube: fresh and lettuce-green from some farm. Even in his youth, Gerry Fuller had never had such an innocent and unworldly appearance. 'Can I help you?' he asked.

'I surely hope so. You are the sheriff here?'

'That I am. What can I do for you?' Fuller chose at the last moment to leave the 'sir' off the end of

118

his question: he hardly thought this young bumpkin rated such a courtesy.

'It's a little difficult. Do you mind if I sit down?'

'You help yourself.' said Fuller, indicating a chair and wondering idly, although without any real apprehension, what the game was. The young man's next words caught him up short and swiftly gained his whole and undivided attention.

'I thought you ought to know that a man near here is running a racket, where he steals cattle and then re-brands them as his own.'

'Why, you don't say so?' said the sheriff. 'How'd you know about this?'

Before entering Oxbow, Dan had given a good deal of thought to what he should and should not tell the authorities. He was certainly not such a cur as to betray the road agents who had rescued him and most likely saved his very life. So they would not feature in his account. Some instinct for self-preservation also warned him that he might be best advised not to mention the men he'd killed either. All things considered, he had decided that the best course of action would be to limit his account to the lynching he had witnessed, and in which he had so very nearly been an active participant, and also what he had learned up at the Barred Os.

While the boy in front of him told his story, haltingly and with a palpable sense of outrage at the injustice he had suffered, Fuller's mind was working frantically, trying to figure out the smartest move now for himself. Of course, if there was a chance of silencing this young fool and somehow disposing of him then that would be the ideal solution. Since first making Dave Carson's acquaintance, he had become pretty reliant upon the money which the rancher handed him each month. It would be a real struggle to do without this supplement to his official salary. On the other hand, if everything was unravelling and Carson was rumbled, then he would be better to go up there now and kill the son of a bitch; then arrest or lynch his associates. It was a tricky decision to have to make so early in the morning.

'You're telling me that you were accused of rustling, is that right?' Fuller asked casually.

'Yes, sir, but it weren't true.'

'Maybe. Maybe not. Accusation like that needs looking into. Tell you what I'm going to do. I'll ride up to this spread and take a look for my own self. Meantime, I'll have to treat you as a material witness, which I'm afraid means keeping you here under lock and key. Hope you understand?'

'Lock me up?' asked Dan in amazement. 'Why, I come here of my own free will to tell you of this!'

'Well, now you told me and it's my business to investigate. I'll have to take that gun you're carrying.'

Young and unused to the ways of the world he might have been, but Dan knew instinctively that there was something amiss here. He was accustomed to trust lawmen, but he had a notion that this man was not as straight as could be wished. Still and all, he had little choice but to surrender his weapon and suffer the sheriff to lock him up in a small, barred enclosure, scarcely bigger than a broom closet, at the back of the office.

CHAPTER 9

It was tolerably obvious to Sheriff Fuller as he set off for the Barred Os that he might need to ditch Carson and his pay-offs, but he wished first to assure himself that there was no way of salvaging the situation. In the meantime, the last thing he needed was that youth roaming around town shooting his mouth off about the Lord only knew what.

Circumstances were combining, quite by chance, to bring matters to a bloody climax. Two hours before Dan Lewis had walked into Fuller's office in Oxbow, a party of twenty men started out from the Triple C. They were led by Ezra Carmichael's nephew Jethro and their intended destination was Dave Carson's place which, at the smart pace they were travelling, they had hopes of reaching before nightfall. On the way, Jethro Carmichael was anxious to overtake his Uncle Ezekiel in order to take counsel with him.

When Gerry Fuller rode into the Barred Os, he

could see at once that everybody there was in a state of high readiness. He had been hailed twice as he approached the place, by men whom he took to be sentries – posted, he assumed, to keep a watch for strangers. This was not at all the usual way of things. So it was that before he'd even spoken with Carson that day, the sheriff had received all the confirmation that he himself required of Dan Lewis's story. It was plain as the nose on your face that trouble was expected at the Barred Os. He observed that Carson himself, contrary to his usual custom, also had a gun at his hip.

'Gerry,' said Dave Carson. 'What brings you up here?' There was an edge to the question. Fuller had picked up his money just the week before and since this was the only dealing that the two men ever had, Carson was probably hinting that the sheriff needn't come more frequently for his hush money.

'Just passing through,' replied Fuller, adding in a lower voice, 'Any chance of a few words alone?'

'I'm kind of busy right now. Can it wait until another day or is it important?'

'I'd say it's pretty important, yeah.'

'All right, come on into the house,' said Carson with an ill grace. 'I hope this won't take long.'

When they were alone in Carson's study, Sheriff Fuller thought that a little plain speaking might be in order. 'First off,' he said, 'is where I don't take kindly to you treating me like some tradesman who's making a nuisance of himself. You can drop that game as soon as you please.'

'What's this all about?'

'Word is, you're in trouble. I'm hearing that your little outfit is about to fall to pieces.'

'The hell you have? Where's you hear such a pack of lies?'

'Never you mind. I got my sources. Why don't we stop foolin' and talk straight. First time I ever see you heeled. You're expectin' a fight, ain't that the way of it?'

Carson didn't reply, but stared moodily out the window. Then he turned back and faced Gerry Fuller squarely. 'You say you want some plain speaking,' he said. 'Well, try this for size. If I go down, I'll take you with me. Others here know you been on the take these eighteen months. Strikes me as you have a powerful strong motive for helping me out now.'

Fuller's eyes narrowed and he shot the owner of the Barred Os an evil look. 'Oh, it's like that, is it?'

'Yes, that's what it's like. You help me out now and I don't say that we can't come to a new arrangement. Maybe more money for you. But I need you on my side this day, else we're both finished.'

'I'll see what I can do,' said Fuller and took his leave without bidding the other man farewell.

'That looks like a drive ahead of us,' said Jethro Carmichael. 'Please God it's my uncle.' He was talking to a man from the Triple C: the closest thing that Carmichael had to a friend. Jethro Carmichael was a moody man of uncertain temper and lacked his uncle's ability to get on effortlessly with all classes and types of men. All his life he'd lived in his Uncle Ezekiel's shadow and never took a step without consulting the old man.

The troop of riders had been on the road since dawn and had progressed at a canter for much of the time; the men vying with each other to see who could be in the lead for the longest period. They most of them knew that there was likely to be some gunplay before night fell, but they were young and keen to display their bravado before their fellows.

'You know anything about this Barred Os place?' asked Jethro of the man at his side.

'Not a damned thing. All I know is it lies nigh to Oxbow, little town off the trail aways.'

'I hope my uncle has some more facts than that. He seemed sure in that letter that this Carson is at the back of all the rustling hereabouts. Lord knows how he found that out while herding steers along the trail.' There was a hint of bitterness in this statement; this being just precisely the kind of information that Ezra Carmichael would be liable to pick up. Even out in the wild and following the Chisholm Trail, his uncle still somehow managed to keep his finger on the pulse and keep a track of what was going on between south Texas and the cow towns of Kansas.

As Jethro Carmichael and his men continued, it became apparent that the cloud of dust reaching up to the sky was indeed a cattle drive. When they overtook it, they found that it was the one which had recently set off from the Three Cs. Almost the first person they saw was old man Carmichael, shouting and swearing like the youngest and most vigorous of the cowboys. Ezra Carmichael's boast was that he never asked any man to do a single thing that he was not ready, willing and able to do his own self; on expeditions such as this present one, he made good his words.

Jethro watched his uncle enviously. There never was such a man for being able to command the respect of others. How he did it was a complete mystery to his nephew. When Ezekiel caught sight of the men, he hailed them boisterously, crying out, 'Don't just sit there like you're a bunch of shop-window dummies! Come on and lend a hand rounding up these damned animals.'

When everybody was covered in dust and had been sworn at and cursed by Ezekiel for being a set of lazy weaklings, he called over his nephew. 'Well boy, you ready for some lively action?'

'I'm not too sure what's what. . . .' began Jethro, before the old man cut in with the greatest irascibility.

'Not sure? What the devil is there to be sure about, I'd like to know? It's all straightforward as can be. This fellow Carson has been preying on us

126

and others for several years now. I may as well tell you, we engaged Pinkerton's to look into it some little while since.'

'Pinkerton's? Why didn't you tell me?'

Ezekiel shrugged. 'Fewer people know about things, the less chance of somebody talking out o' turn. Anyways, I ain't yet got their report, but my information's sound enough. We ride down on that Carson's place, the Barred Os, tonight and then if we can find anything don't look right, why, I'll see him hanged.'

Jethro was appalled. 'Lord a mercy, Uncle, you can't do that! What are you thinking of?'

'Who says I can't?' demanded the old man pugnaciously. 'That's the law o' the range. I'll warrant Carson knows that as well as I do. I'm telling you once for all, I won't be put upon. If this man's been behind all them stock thefts, then I'll have his life.'

'Anyways,' continued Ezra Carmichael, 'I ain't about to ask you to do the job. I'm a-comin' along, you know.'

'It's not to be thought of, Uncle Ezekiel. Let me notify the sheriff in the nearest town. Let's do this legal. Please!'

But Jethro knew his uncle well enough to see that his mind was made up. For good or ill, the old man was utterly determined to settle this affair in his own way and by his own rules. The only problem was that Ezra Carmichael followed the old frontier code and this would not always answer now in the modern world. Launching what was, to all intents and purposes, an armed raid like this could have serious consequences for them all. Still, his uncle was not a man to be gainsaid and if he said he'd do a thing, then by God he'd do it, or die in the attempt.

It was lonely and dull in the little cell and Dan Lewis thought he'd go clean out of his mind if he had to stay there much longer. In the story-books which Dan had read, mainly trashy dime novels, men locked up in cells always seemed to pace up and down restlessly. There was barely room enough here, though, to stand up and step to the zinc bucket which had been provided for his bodily needs. He was certainly unable to take more than one pace before reaching either the wall or the iron bars which stretched from ceiling to floor. He'd no idea what time it was now, but guessed from the height of the sun outside the tiny barred window that it couldn't be far off noon.

When he heard the key turning in the door leading to the street, Dan couldn't help calling out, hoping that his imprisonment was about to end. 'All right,' said Sheriff Fuller, 'just hold your horses there. We got all the time in the world.' He went over to the stove and fiddled around there for a spell, before setting a coffee pot on top. Then he came over to the cell and said, 'I'm not at all sure that I'm doing the right thing, but I feel in a good mood today.' Then he unlocked the door and indicated that Dan could come out.

'I'm free to go?'

'Not so fast. We need to have a few words together first. Sit down. Happen you'd like some coffee?'

'Yes, please.'

Fuller prepared two cups of black coffee and then settled down behind his desk. He said, 'I've got my doubts about you, but all things considered, I'm minded to release you. On condition, that is, as you leave Oxbow and head straight back to your own town. Indian Falls, wasn't it?'

'That's right. But what about the rustling?'

'That ain't your affair. You get yourself home and be thankful as nobody sees fit to charge you.'

'Charge me? What with?' asked Dan indignantly.

'Rustling. Now I'm going to give you back your gun, your horse is still outside and you can just dig up and head south. What d'you say?'

It was perfectly clear to Dan Lewis that there was something about this that wasn't open and above board. Was this shifty-looking individual part of the racket that was being run up at the Barred Os? One thing was for sure, this man was not playing straight with him; which was a shocking thought to a young man who had always had the healthiest respect for the law. He said, 'That's right kind of you, sir. I'll go straight home, you can depend on it.'

129

In point of fact, Gerry Fuller didn't really want the boy to go home at all. He was right ticked off with Carson and hadn't taken to being threatened in that way with exposure. As far as he was able to apprehend, Carson was anticipating some species of assault on his place and was readying himself for a regular siege. That was all well and good; the sheriff hoped devoutly that a band of marauders descended on the Barred Os and killed every mother's son to be found there. At the very least, the sooner that Dave Carson ceased to breathe, the happier that he, Fuller, would be. He had more or less resigned himself to receiving no further pay-offs, which was a pity. Still, there were worse things than having to depend exclusively upon his salary from the post of sheriff. Not having even that salary, for instance, would be the devil of a thing.

The way Sheriff Fuller had the case reasoned out, the more men there were gunning for Dave Carson, the better the chances of his being killed and nobody ever finding out about the cosy little arrangement that the two of them had enjoyed. This young fellow didn't look like he'd be any great shakes with a gun, but he had a grudge against Carson and whatever he promised now, he was sure to go haring off up to the Barred Os just as soon as Fuller turned him loose.

'Well, boy,' said Fuller, 'have we got us a deal?'

'Surely,' said Dan. 'I'm going to mount up and ride back home at once.'

130

For a moment, Sheriff Fuller was tempted to laugh out loud. Here the two of them were, both lying their heads off and neither one of them meaning a damned word that he said and both determined to put one over the other. In the event, he restrained himself and said simply, 'All right, get on out of here and don't let me catch a sight of you again.'

Although he was often short with the man and frequently berated him for falling down on the job, Dave Carson had never felt the need for Fats's help so keenly as he did that day. Not only that, he could really have done with the other nine men who had ridden off with his foreman. God knew what had become of those ten men; it was as if they had vanished from the face of the earth.

There were twelve men living and working at the Barred Os, but only nine of them could be relied upon if things got ugly. The other three were weaklings who, in Carson's estimation, would be no use in any sort of rough house. He was handy enough with a rifle himself and so that gave them ten guns with which to defend the place. The advantage always lay with the defenders in such situations and so Dave Carson was reasonably confident that he would be able to fight off some cowboy lynch mob. Provided of course that Sheriff Fuller didn't involve himself by deputizing a bunch of men from Oxbow and turning up here on his own account. Carson was

131

under no illusions at all on this subject; there was going to be a reckoning between him and Fuller and that sooner rather than later. For now, though, he needed to organize the defence of his property against the men who, if the Pinkerton's agent had been telling the truth, were even now riding towards him.

'You two men,' Carson called across the yard, 'you want to fall foul of this lynch mob alone? Otherwise, get rifles and go and join the men over at the main gate. We don't stand together, we'll all hang together.'

'Yes, boss,' mumbled the men, with no great show of enthusiasm, and went off to arm themselves. They were two of the three that Carson hadn't thought he could rely upon and he was pleased to see that they did not look to be leaving, but preferred to take their chances with the rest of them. Depending upon the size of the gang heading that way, this was like to be a close-run thing and every extra gun was welcome and could tilt the matter in their favour.

Three men had been posted up on the high ground to the west of the Barred Os. There was no doubt that any trouble was going to be coming from the south, but as a precaution, Carson had set another man to watch the road to Oxbow. He didn't trust Gerry Fuller one little bit and now that they'd had sharp words, Carson wanted to be sure that he would see any group of riders starting towards them from town.

As far as the owner of the Barred Os could make out, they should be in a good position to see off up to twenty or thirty attackers. After all, they were forewarned and forearmed; not to mention they knew the terrain a sight better than those seeking to do them harm. Despite the danger, Carson felt quite buoyed up and optimistic. This wasn't, after all, the first bit of danger that they had encountered while running this show. He'd have to patch things up with the sheriff of Oxbow after this was all over, maybe raise his share of the profits a little, but that apart, Dave Carson was confident enough. To the outside world, even in Oxbow, it would all look like some squabble between two cattle outfits. Who would be able to say who was in the right and which was the villain of the piece?

Jethro Carmichael was in despair. He knew, had known for almost the whole of his life, that his Uncle Ezekiel was stubborn as an ox, but this was something else again. He tried once more to make the old man see sense.

'Uncle, it isn't to be thought of! Why don't you go along now with those steers and I promise to handle this for you.'

'Handle it?' asked his uncle, scornfully. 'You mean you'll be kissing and making up with that bastard and asking him to pledge his word not to take any more of our cattle. No, this needs a sharp lesson and I'm the man to deliver it.'

'You could end up on the wrong side of the law,' pointed out Jethro. 'It's just not worth the risk at your age.'

'At my age?' said Ezra Carmichael, raising his head like a rattler about to strike. 'At my age? My age be damned to you. I said I'll lead this foray and by God that's just what I mean to do.'

The sun had only lately set and the two of them were standing apart from the others. Jethro was speaking in a low and confidential tone of voice, but his uncle, who got deafer every year, was practically bellowing his defiance. There was no point in aggravating the old man further and so his nephew said, 'Well, you have it your own way.'

'You're damned right I will!'

After riding south for a mile or so, until he was out of sight of the town, Dan Lewis headed to his left and then circled round Oxbow in the direction that he guessed led to the Barred Os. He didn't know himself just what he would do when he got there, but he wasn't about to let this end in such a vague and inconclusive fashion with the slur of having been detected in the act of rustling still hanging over his head.

The last few days had been an education for the young man. He had almost been hanged, killed his first man and then been locked up in a cell as well. A grown man might have found this dizzying succession of new experiences alarming and

134

disconcerting; but when you are young, you often just take such things in your stride. Dan supposed that at some stage, he would need to sit down and think all this over carefully, but for now he was only keen to clear his name. Fretting about having killed men could wait until he got back to Indian Falls.

While he was musing in this way, Dan didn't notice the man perched on a rock, away over to his left. The first he knew was that somebody shouted to him, 'Where are you going?'

'Nowhere especial,' replied Dan, not being minded to discuss his affairs with a complete stranger. 'Why're you askin'?'

'I'm watching out for any strangers heading this way. Meaning such as might be looking for trouble.'

'Well, I sure ain't looking for any trouble,' said Dan pleasantly. 'Who set you to stand guard?'

The man stood up and came down the slope, so that he could talk with Dan at a normal, conversational level. He said, 'Fellow called Carson. I picked up with his boys a week ago, but seems he's running into difficulties. As between the two of us, I ain't all that sure as I'm a-going to be stickin' around much longer.'

'That so?'

'Yes, siree. Say, you headin' up to the Barred Os?'

'The Barred Os?' Dan assumed a mystified expression. 'What's that?'

'Did I not say? That's the spread I'm working for.'

'No, I don't reckon as I'm heading that way. I'm

aiming to cut across the Chisholm Trail. I'm on the right path for that, ain't I?'

'That you are. Just keep going straight. You might want to cut along to the left a mite. There's another fellow setting watch and he might not ask you first what your business is.'

'Thanks for the tip. Well, I hope it all goes well for you.'

'Thanks, stranger. You take care now.'

CHAPTER 10

Sheriff Fuller waited for an hour, by which time he was quite sure that the boy he had lately released would be well on his way to the Barred Os. Then he went to a stout, locked closet in one corner of his office that he called his 'armoury' and opened it. He selected a Volcanic repeating rifle, which he'd found to be a faithful and reliable companion during the late war. Then he broke open a box of cartridges and filled his pockets with the shiny brass shells. It would do no harm at all to be prepared for a violent confrontation. All else apart, he might get the chance of a shot at that bastard Carson. After their meeting that day, Sheriff Fuller was of the decided opinion that Dave Carson would be better under the ground, rather than walking above it and spreading a heap of unsavoury tales about Oxbow's sheriff.

There is no telling how the subsequent events might have unfolded, if Gerry Fuller had been able to reach the Barred Os alive. It was his misfortune, though, to encounter the same jittery man with whom Dan Lewis had exchanged words a while earlier. In the intervening half hour, dusk had fallen and it was increasingly hard to make out whom you were dealing with in the gloom. Fuller heard a man shout at him, 'Throw down your weapons, you hear what I tell you?'

Instinctively, such a challenge caused Fuller to reach out the rifle from the scabbard at front of the saddle. It might have been virtually night-time and the man on the ridge above him could see only the vaguest shadows, but the aggressive nature of the movement was hard to mistake and a shot rang out.

'Ah, shit!' exclaimed Fuller, as he fell from his horse. He was more vexed than anything else. The wound itself was a clean one which had cut a furrow through his upper arm and after bandaging would heal up after a week or so. He lay there winded and unable to move for a few seconds. The man who had shot him came loping down to see who he'd hit. When he recognized Sheriff Fuller, his dismay was comical to behold. Leastways, it would have been comical, had Sheriff Fuller's first instinct not been to bluster and threaten.

'Gee, Sheriff,' said the fellow, who had met Fuller in Oxbow's one and only saloon, three days earlier, 'I'm real sorry. I'd no idea it was you. I wouldn't o' shot you for anything.'

'Would you not, you stupid whore's son?' said

Fuller wrathfully. 'I tell you now, you'll hang for this!'

'Hang?' responded the fellow, horrified and alarmed. 'It was purely an accident.'

'No matter for that,' said Fuller. 'You'll hang all the same, for the attempted murder of a peace officer.' The sheriff didn't mean this, of course. He was in pain and mightily displeased at being shot off his horse by this slow-witted oaf. Had he left it at that, things might still have passed off without any serious harm being done, but Fuller was so angry that he opened his mouth just that little bit too wide, saying, 'Don't think as I don't know who you are. I recall you well enough from the Golden Eagle. Your name's Provis.'

There was silence and then the man standing over him said slowly, 'Ah, you recollect my name, then?' Until Fuller had spoken his name out loud, Albert Provis had been hoping that the sheriff might not know him from Adam. Hearing his name, though, combined with the threat of facing the hangman for what Provis saw as a simple, regrettable but understandable mistake on his part put a different complexion on the matter. Provis thought for a second and then said, 'That's a horse of a different colour.' He drew the pistol at his hip and shot Gerry Fuller twice in the chest, saying as he did so, 'Dead men tell no tales, or so they say.'

Having, as he saw it, saved himself from the immediate danger of being hanged, it remained only for Albert Provis to extricate himself from the little matter of having killed a man. He was, according to his simple way of seeing the thing, in a much better position now than he had been before, when Sheriff Fuller had only been wounded. At that time, there had been a witness who looked only too ready and willing to testify against him in a court of law. Now, the one person who knew what he had done was lying dead in front of him. It remained for Provis only to do what he had done a dozen times before in his vagabond life, which was to mount up and ride hell for leather away from the scene of his latest misdeed.

When the attack on the Barred Os came, it was bloody and sudden. One of the men watching the track leading in the direction of the Chisholm Trail heard the rumble of hoofs and from the sound of them, suspected that a sizable body of riders were heading his way. He listened for a half-minute more and then ran to his horse, intending to ride off and raise the alarm. He couldn't have known what a wily old devil Ezra Carmichael was, though. The old man was a veteran of the Mexican War and sundry other campaigns against the Indians. He wasn't about to take any chances in a venture of this nature and so had put out flankers: outriders who would scout ahead of the main body.

Carson's sentry was scarcely in the saddle, before he heard a stern voice requesting him to throw down his gun and consider himself a captive. He figured that if he made no warlike moves and simply ignored this command, then he would be able to gallop back and join his friends. After all, what were the odds of somebody shooting him in the back? In truth, the odds were nigh-on as certain as could be, because Carmichael had given orders that nobody was to be allowed to escape. The man who had issued the challenge also had a powerful motive for not allowing this fellow to flee, because it is always a sight easier and more pleasant when attacking armed men to take them quite by surprise; rather than have them waiting for you with their pieces cocked and ready.

The element of surprise was somewhat reduced by this ruthless action because, although the pistol shots which had killed Gerry Fuller had not been heard back at the Barred Os, the sound of a rifle carries further and the distant crack was remarked by those clustered round in front of the big house.

'Hark to that,' said Carson, when he heard the shot. 'It came from yonder, up towards the trail.' He had already laid his plans and sent off a party of six men to cover the approach from the west.

Dave Carson was pleased that so far he had had no desertions at all. There was a strong element of self-interest involved in the men working for him. They all knew by now about the men who had been lynched up on the trail and not a one of them wanted to take the risk of being taken alone. At least this way, if they all fought together, there was a sporting chance that they might survive. Things had reached such a pass now that if the men from the Carmichael Cattle Company caught any stragglers from the Barred Os, then they would be like to hang them out of hand.

The men who left the vicinity of the house at the first sound of shooting were carrying rifles. Their aim was to position themselves on either side of the track leading to the Barred Os and harry the attackers with sniper fire. This would give the main force of defenders the opportunity to get into good spots to fight off the men from the Three Cs. As is so often the case with plans of battle, things didn't go at all as was hoped or expected. For one thing, the men from the Triple C were coming on at a far greater speed than was thought likely. The assumption had been that they would advance tentatively, taking their time lest opposition was encountered. In fact, they rode in at a canter and so the two groups collided in the darkness. There was confusion, swearing and a brief exchange of fire, before the six men sent by Carson realized that they were outnumbered by better than three to one and fled back the way they had come. Typically for skirmishes in pitch darkness, not a single ball found its mark.

After passing the sentry, Dan Lewis had dismounted and led his horse quietly along the way leading to the Barred Os. It was dark, but even so he felt horribly exposed. If there had been one man with a gun keeping watch, why not two or three? At any moment, he expected to hear the sound of a shot and feel a Minie ball slamming into his chest. But, being young, the fear of death was by way of being an abstraction, rather than a tangible risk. When you are seventeen, you know that you are not really going to die.

There were voices ahead and so Dan halted and tried to work out the best plan of action. He didn't even know why he had come here like this, let alone what he might be about to do next. His aim was to clear his name and having not had any satisfaction from the sheriff of Oxbow, he knew that he was obliged to take matters into his own hands, but the good Lord alone knew what that was like to mean in practice. Maybe his coming haring up here like this was no more than a fool's errand; a mad snipe hunt which would end in failure.

From some way behind him, Dan Lewis heard a faint pop, followed a minute later by two more. What these portended, other than the obvious fact that some folk back there were at outs with each other, he didn't know. Then there was a more distinct shot in the direction he was heading. That was a rifle, for sure, he reasoned.

There was a lightning-blasted tree standing nearby, its bare branches gaunt against the night sky. Dan tethered his horse to this tree and continued on foot. The sound of voices grew louder and then he heard in the distance what was unmistake-ably the sound of a short, sharp gun battle. The worst of it was that he had no idea what was going on. It was tolerably certain that somebody or other was attacking the Barred Os, but who that might be was anybody's guess. I sure hope, the boy thought to himself, that I don't get taken for one of them rustlers. That would be the very devil of a thing to occur.

The twenty cowboys of the Triple C hit the ranch like a hammer blow; they punched through the men posted around the corrals, who were in theory the first line of defence. Two of the riders were killed, but their momentum was such that there was little time for any of the others to take heed of this. The horsemen swept past, on towards the house. There was sporadic gunfire from Carson's men crouching behind the bales of hay and low stone walls, but at the sight of so many riders galloping down on them, the defenders cut and ran. They had, after all, no strong personal stake in the preser-vation of Dave Carson's enterprise, being, when all was said and done, just hired hands. Now that the storm was upon them and they could see a bunch of angry men intent on tackling a gang of rustlers, each man thought only of his own neck. As Carson watched, his little band of warriors melted away into the darkness.

Dave Carson had been in tight spots more than once in his life and always in the past he had managed somehow to wriggle out of them and live to fight another day. As far as the owner of the Barred Os was concerned, this was just one more such day. Most of his wealth was invested in banks and much as it pained him, he acknowledged that the loss of the big house behind him, which he could see burning down, wouldn't be the ruination of him; he had enough cash stashed away to start again somewhere, albeit on a more modest scale. The question now was how to make his getaway.

From behind a tree, Dan Lewis watched events as the men who had ridden into the ranch, where he had lately stayed, mopped up the opposition. There was the occasional demand for some man to throw down his weapon, but the commonest sound was the crackle of shots as the men who had been defending the Barred Os were picked off one by one. There didn't seem any sort of wish on the part of the attackers to be burdened with prisoners. Although he was pleased enough to see the rustlers who had almost caused him to lose his own life being dealt with, there was a twinge of regret as well, because it looked increasingly likely that at this rate, Dan would never have the chance to clear his name.

Having reached this melancholy conclusion, Dan Lewis thought that the best thing he could do would be simply to stay right there behind that tree, out of sight of everybody, and wait for things to die down a little until he could see a chance of slipping away quietly and without drawing any attention to himself. It was a darn shame, but there it was. With this operation being broken up now, he would most likely have to learn to live with the stigma of having once been suspected of being involved in stock theft. As he was mulling over this unpalatable state of affairs to himself, Dan saw the man who he had been introduced to as the leader of this outfit, Dave Carson, skulking in the nearby shadows. From what he could see, nobody else had yet noticed the man in all the confusion.

Two impulses contended for mastery in Dan's breast. On the one hand, he surely would hate to see the man who had ultimately been to blame for all the fixes in which Dan had found himself over the last few days escaping scot-free. On the other, though, he didn't feel inclined to draw any attention to his own self, lest he be identified with, and share the fate of, the members of this nest of thieves and rustlers. There's no telling how this dilemma might have resolved itself if the man he was watching had simply vanished into the dark night. What actually happened was that Dan heard a man shout urgently, 'There's one o' them! Catch a-hold of him, there.'

For a moment, Dan was affeared that he had himself been spotted by the raiders, but then he realized with satisfaction that it was the owner of the Barred Os who had been seen. Dan waited curiously to see what would befall the fellow now that he had been flushed from cover.

You could say many sharp and uncomplimentary things about Dave Carson, but nobody had ever accused him of cowardice. There were some men who might have been tempted to turn tail and run in such a tight situation. Not Carson, though. Because almost at the same instant that he heard that shout, drawing attention to his presence, Carson saw a way out of the trap. On more than one occasion, he had met Ezra Carmichael socially and he had already marked the old man as directing operations personally against the Barred Os. Carmichael was sitting on his horse by a tree, only a dozen yards away from where Carson had been trying to slip away unmarked. Before anybody could have guessed what he was about, Carson sprinted up to where the owner of the Triple C was sitting, looking hugely smug and satisfied with himself, and hauled him right down on to the ground.

Old as he was, Carmichael was as lithe and angry as a mountain lion and furious at having such liberties taken with his person. Not apparently even stunned by being grabbed from the saddle and dumped unceremoniously on to the ground, he whirled round, his hand snaking down to the pistol at his hip, but Dave Carson was too quick for him. His own gun was in his hand and cocked and just as Ezra Carmichael's hand closed over the hilt of his pistol, he felt the touch of cold metal to his neck and a deadly voice informed him, 'Draw that weapon and I blow out your brains right this

147

second.' Carson paused, to give his words time to sink in, and then said, 'Tell all your men to draw back. Do it now or you're as good as dead.'

'All of you move back,' called Carmichael. 'Right back out of the way. This bastard's got the drop on me and I ain't fixin' to die just yet awhiles.' Some of his men seemed reluctant to abandon their boss and Ezra Carmichael roared at them, 'Do as you're damned well bid, will you? Any man as don't do as I say can consider himself dismissed.' All the men moved back.

'Right now, Mr Carmichael,' said Carson quietly, 'here's how we're going to work this. You and me are going for a little ride together. I'm going to remove your gun,' saying which, Carson suited the action to the words and took the old man's gun from its holster, throwing it to one side, 'then we're going to walk together, with your horse, over to the barn there. All the time, we're going to keep so close, we might kiss each other. Not, you understand, because of any personal charms you might hold for me, but to discourage one of your fellows from trying to shoot me. Closer we are together, less likely that anybody'll run the risk.'

'And then?' asked Carmichael, his voice icy cold with contempt. 'I suppose you'll shoot me anyway when we're clear of here.'

'Not a bit of it. What a mistrustful and suspicious man you are! No, we'll ride for a couple of hours and then, always providing that I think we haven't been followed, I'll let you go and then make my own way off.'

'You won't get away with this,' said Carmichael.

'Oh, I think I will. Come on, let's get moving. Nice and slowly over to the barn there.' It was at that precise moment that Dan Lewis, who was only a dozen feet from the other two men and had heard every word of this discussion, sprang into action.

CHAPTER 11

Dave Carson was in a pretty confident state of mind. All Carmichael's men were a good distance away and he was that close to the old man that not one of them could have risked loosing off a shot at him without the very real risk of killing their boss instead. As long as Ezra Carmichael believed that he was going to live, then he would almost certainly make his men swear not to launch any pursuit and just to set tight here until he returned. Not that Dave Carson had any intention of letting the man go free, of course. This old devil had wrecked one of the sweetest little rackets that Carson had ever heard tell of and it wasn't in reason that he should be allowed to get away with that. Still, the important thing was that Carmichael *believed* that he was going to live. Old men are exceedingly tenacious of life and worry about death a sight more than youngsters.

Where the man came from who sprang upon

him, knocking the gun from his hand, Carson could not have said. He would have taken an oath that there was nobody closer to him and Carmichael than fifty or sixty feet. He clubbed the old man in the neck, as hard as he could, with his clenched fist and had the satisfaction of seeing Carmichael keel over, temporarily out of action. Then he turned to face his assailant.

Carson knew the boy at once – it was that young fellow whom Fats had brought back after the lynching, the one who had probably killed Garcia. These thoughts flashed through his mind, even as he was moving, diving to the ground for the gun which had been dashed from his grasp.

Whatever had been in the young man's mind when he jumped the owner of the Barred Os, whether just to rescue the old man or knock out Dave Carson and surrender him up to justice, once Carson went scrabbling around for his pistol, it was inevitable that there would be an exchange of fire.

As soon as Dan saw the man dive down for his gun, he drew his own pistol, cocking the hammer with his thumb as he did so. His sole immediate aim in leaping into action had been to rescue the kind-looking old man from the person he knew to be the head of a gang of ruthless criminals, but having done so, he could see that it was now life and death and that if he did nothing, why, this fellow would surely gun him down. Even so, he waited, hoping that it wouldn't come to that.

His reluctance to kill a man might have been commendable enough in its own way, but it was very nearly the death of Dan Lewis. While he stood there like a fool, a cocked pistol in his hand, Carson had snatched up his own piece and was turning to face the boy. There was only a split second in it, but Dan's shot hit the other man in the chest. Carson had already begun to squeeze the trigger and when the ball took him through the heart, he clenched his hand reflexively, causing him to fire. His aim was spoiled by being hit, but his ball wasn't completely wasted. It flew straight at Dan Lewis's head, catching him a glancing blow on his right temple which felt like somebody had whacked him hard with a hickory stick.

As Dan sank to his knees, the sickening pain almost depriving him of his senses, he was aware of men rushing up to the old man, who drove them off with angry cries of, 'Never mind fussing round me, you bunch of old women! Look to that young fellow and see what's needful.' Then, for the first time in his life, Dan Lewis fainted.

When he came round, Dan found that somebody was examining his forehead critically. This man said, 'I never saw a closer thing! A quarter inch to one side and it would have broken his skull to pieces.'

A querulous voice that he recognized as belonging to the old man whose aid he had gone to said, 'You mean he'll live?'

'Live? He's fine as you like. Might have a

152

headache, but nothing worse. You can see for your-self: the ball grazed his skin, but nothing worse. Luckiest escape I ever seed in the whole course of my life.'

'Thank God!' said the old man piously. 'Thank God!'

At this point, Dan opened his eyes and said, 'I'm right sorry to be a nuisance to you folk.'

'Hush your mouth, you damned fool,' said the old man, who was bending over him solicitously. 'You saved my life.'

'You sure he weren't one o' them?' said another man, standing nearby. 'Lord knows what he was doing, hidin' behind that there tree.'

'I don't much care if he's one of Satan's imps,' said Ezra Carmichael irritably, 'he saved my life and nearly paid for the privilege with his own. You all hush up now!'

Dan tried to sit up. The movement made his head feel as though it was exploding and he almost vomited, but now or never was his opportunity to set things straight. 'Steady now, son,' said the old man at his side, putting a hand on Dan's shoulder. 'You shouldn't ought to be moving.'

'I'm all right, sir. Just a mite groggy, is all. I want to explain to you and the others what I was doing, hiding behind that tree.'

'There's no need. . . .'

'Sorry to be contrary-wise, sir, but there's every need!'

So it was that sitting there in the darkness, with a ring of interested listeners hanging upon his every word, Dan Lewis let spill the whole story of his adventures since signing up as a wrangler for the Three Cs. It took a little while to tell the entire tale, but nobody interrupted him. After he'd finished speaking, Ezra Carmichael stretched himself, shot the boy a keen glance and said, 'That sounds to me like the God's honest truth.' There were nods and grunts of agreement.

'I just wanted to make sure everybody knows as I ain't any sort o' thief,' said Dan. 'So if that's all plain, I guess I can go back to Indian Falls.'

'Not so hasty,' said Carmichael. 'You may not know it, but the Triple C belongs to me. 'Fore this all blew up, I was running five hundred head o' cattle north along the Chisholm Trail. We're going clear up to Elsworth. Can't recompense you none for all you been through, but if you want to earn a dollar a day as a wrangler when we set off again tomorrow, well, the job's yours.'

So it was that after what might be called a false start, Dan Lewis set off the next day with Ezra Carmichael and his men; driving half a thousand steers up to the railhead at Elsworth.

The work was hard and in those eight weeks, Dan laboured a good deal harder than he ever had on the farm back home. He surely earned that sixty dollars by the time they finally reached Elsworth. Now, it wasn't old Ezra Carmichael's way to show

154

emotion or give any indication of favouring one man over another and he yelled and cursed at Dan when they were on the trail every whit as much as he did the others. Nevertheless, the old man had taken a liking to the boy: something over and above the gratitude a man might properly feel towards somebody who has saved his life.

In some ways, Dan was a little sad when they finally hit Elsworth. Being in a cow town was certainly a novel and exciting experience, but he knew that pretty soon now, he would have to be making tracks back to Indian Falls. It had all been a great adventure, but it wasn't real life. That consisted of feeding hogs and picking stones out of the fields. He'd enjoyed the last eight weeks, but now it was time to return to his normal life. Still and all, the memory of those weeks, especially the first few days, would stay with him all his life.

The day after they reached Elsworth and had herded the steers into the holding pens in the yard by the railroad depot, Mr Carmichael sought out Dan, ostensibly in order to thank him one final time for saving his life. In fact, there was more to it than that. After some preliminary remarks about the satisfactory way in which the boy had conducted himself on the trail and various such things, the old man said, 'So you'll be heading back to Indian Falls now, is that about the strength of it?'

'Yes, sir. What else would I do?'

Generally, once the younger men were paid off at

the end of the drive, they went on the spree and then returned to their homes and took up their ordinary lives again. A few went off to work at various ranches, but these were the exceptions.

They were standing by the pens, the lowing of the cattle making it hard to sustain a conversation at normal levels. Carmichael said, 'You're a good worker. I could find a use for somebody like you back at the Triple C. Not just for a few months here and there. I mean a good, steady job. Pay you well.'

Dan was touched by this and could see that the old man did not want to part from him. Whether Dan reminded him of his son, killed in the war, or perhaps for some other reason, Ezra Carmichael was definitely reluctant to end their association. It was a delicate situation and Dan thought carefully for a space before answering.

'It's right nice of you, sir. If I was going to work any place, then I guess that the Three Cs would be the one I'd choose, for a bet. But it won't answer.'

'Oh? How's that?'

'I almost didn't come up here this year. My pa's dead and there's only me and my ma most o' the time. I mean, we have hired men to help and all, but half of them is hardly worth the money we pay 'em.'

Carmichael nodded, understandingly. 'Isn't that the truth,' he said. 'I'm a man who speaks from bitter experience. Number o' useless types I've hired in my time.'

156

'Anyways,' continued the boy, 'I don't like to leave Ma by herself, just relyin' on those fellows. It ain't manly, if you take my meaning. It's my place now to be there, looking after her interests and tending to what needs doin'. Not but that I wouldn't like to work for you, Mr Carmichael. Truth to tell, there's nothing I'd like better. But it would kind o' seem like running out on my own kin and that's not a thing to be done, not no-how.'

For a minute or so, Mr Carmichael said nothing and Dan wondered if the old man were going deaf and hadn't heard all he had said because of the noise in the stockyards. Then Carmichael said, 'You're in the right, son. Family's the most important thing in the world and a man who neglects his duties in that direction ain't a real man at all. Still and all, I'm sorry that we got to part. I watched you on the trail. You got the makings of a good man. Let me tell you, any time you want a job, just let me know, 'fore you start hiring yourself out elsewhere.'

'There ain't nobody I'd sooner work for, sir,' said Dan sincerely.

Two days later, Dan Lewis saddled up and rode south out of Elsworth. It wouldn't take him any two months to get back to Indian Falls, but it was still a thousand miles between him and home. He had begun to worry about whether that new fellow was up to the job. When all was said and done, he'd looked to Dan like some worn out saddle-bum and he was feeling a mite guilty for coming off on this jaunt, for all that his Ma had represented it as the thing to do.

One thing that exercised Dan greatly as he was travelling back to Texas was how much of what had befallen him he should tell his mother. On the one hand, he didn't take to the notion of concealing anything from his ma, but on the other; she would just about have a blue fit if he told her the half of what had happened to him since last he had seen her. In the end, he thought that he would kind of take his cue from her and answer questions in a straightforward way, while not volunteering over-much information.

In the event, Dan needn't have fretted about hiding anything from his mother. She had grown up with five brothers and in her experience, as soon as a young man of seventeen years of age is out of sight of his home all manner of hell is likely to break loose. The second she set eyes upon her son, she could see at once that he had changed. The precise details didn't worry her, the fact was that he had left a boy and come back a man. Well, that was very right and proper.

'Well, boy,' she greeted him, 'you sure took your time about coming home. What you been doin', picking flowers along the way or something?'

'I came straight back, Ma, just as soon as we settled those beasts in the pens at Elsworth.'

'Well, I won't deny as I'm glad to see you back again. That fellow I engaged is about as much use as. . . . Well, I don't know what use he is, to speak plainly. Now that you've condescended to rejoin us, happen you'd like to give him his marching orders?'

This was a development which Dan could not have foreseen. His mother had always been very ready to send any of the hired hands packing, if they failed to meet her very exacting standards. That she should delegate such a task to her son indicated some shift in their relationship and the way in which she viewed him. He said nothing, but inwardly rejoiced.

Later that day, after he had intimated to the help that it was about time he thought of moving on, as his services at the Lewis farm were no longer needed, Dan walked round the fields and examined the outbuildings. It struck him that there was plenty of work needed to be done around the place. He hadn't realized before just how much he had been taking on himself in the last year and what a difference it had made, his not being there for eight weeks. That sort of trip was a luxury that he would not be able to afford in future. There was a heap of work needed to be done and if he didn't do it, who would?

That evening, Dan talked over with his mother some of the little jobs he had noticed that needed to be tackled. She said, 'Well, don't come a-troublin' me with 'em all. Strikes me that if you know what's to be done, you might as well just get on and do it. You ain't a child any more, you know. There's no call to tell me every little thing you propose to do.'

It seemed to the young man that his mother was passing over a good chunk of the management of this little farm to him. Why, she had all but told him that he was in charge now! Dan felt a little guilty that he had not yet told his mother of the scrapes he'd been in on the trail. He said, 'Ma, you ain't asked me aught of what happened over the last two months. You want I should tell you?'

'A heap of foolishness, I'll be bound,' said his mother. 'Men fighting and being killed and you in and out o' trouble. That about cover it?'

Dan laughed. 'Pretty much.' He felt a sudden rush of love for his mother and he went over to her and kissed the top of her head.

'Lord, child,' she exclaimed, 'what are you about? You ain't going silly, I hope?'

'No, Ma, not a bit of it.'

'Well, that's a mercy, at any rate. 'Stead o' sitting here jawin', there's them hogs to feed. Or are you too grand for that now?'

'No, I ain't too grand for to feed the hogs,' he said, and went out with a good-natured smile on his face to find the swill bucket. It surely was good to be home.